The O'Neil
A Novel

Gene McTiernan

THE O'NEIL

Copyright © 2024 Gene McTiernan

This is a work of fiction. All Rights Reserved. No part of this publication may be reproduced or transmitted in any form or by any means, electronic, digital or mechanical, including photocopying, scanning, digitizing, recording or any information storage or retrieval system, without written permission from the copyright holder.

ISBN 979-8-9901904-2-9

Printed in the United States of America
Minuteman Press Berkeley

A NOVEL

For

Evelyn,

Chloe,

the Owl,

and

the Bees

THE O'NEIL

The Birth

"*Pog mo thoin!*[1] Oh, *pog mo thoin!*" Marianne O'Neil (née Donegan) yelled with each contraction. She was not one to use the curse words, so this was as bad as her speech ever got. "*Pog mo thoin!*" was the expletive she regularly relied upon; she used it for every occasion whether it fit the situation or not. It could be anger, it could be excitement, it could be pain or even joy. Sometimes she sprinkled a modifier in front of it, such as "Well" or "Oh." The modifier sometimes made it easier for listeners to determine her meaning, but not always. She reserved the modifier for special events, such as, in this case, delivering a breech baby, which certainly qualified as one of those times.

At the business end of this intense scene sat Martha, the midwife, a usually jovial and calm middle-aged woman who served as midwife throughout County Wicklow. With each contraction the view from her eyes revealed the baby's arse peek out from the birth canal. The confluence of what she saw and what she heard from Marianne was enough to make anyone laugh out loud. She would have laughed were it not for the fact that she alone was responsible for delivering this breech baby. Delivering the babe in an isolated Irish cottage in the middle of County Wicklow made it even less funny. This, coupled with the fact that she had not slept in nearly twenty-four hours, took away any joy from the moment. Martha, as well as John and Marianne, knew there was a high risk of this babe dying during delivery and that Marianne's labor was going to be much more painful than a typical delivery.

---

[1] "Kiss my arse."

There was mayhem inside the cottage, but outside lay the peaceful green countryside at the foot of the Wicklow Mountains. The stone cottage blended into the rocks scattered about the base of Mount Kippure, and the thickly thatched roof resembled a small field ready to be turned. Peat smoke rose from the chimney sticking above the thatch from the large hearth below. The cottage was embraced in a blanket of early-morning mist rising slowly to join the peat smoke above.

"Come on, Marianne," she said as she wiped sweat off her forehead. "You can do this, lass." Her senses were so heightened from the stress of this event that she swore she could hear the sweat squeezing from the pores of her skin as well as the dust settling on the windowpanes.

"*Pog mo thoin!*" was the only reply.

"Arse, *pog mo thoin!*" "Arse, *pog mo thoin!*" The distressed cries continued for what seemed like a very long time. It was almost as if the outbursts were choreographed, or more likely, Martha's tired brain was playing tricks on her. The scene was like a strange dream. Martha now wondered what John O'Neil might be thinking as he waited with nervous anticipation in the kitchen. She knew he was aware of the potential disaster of a breech birth, for both mother and infant. She whispered prayers for divine help between Marianne's contractions.

With some more words of encouragement by Martha and an urgent push by Marianne, the baby's bottom was ejected from the birth canal. Martha's nimble fingers quickly freed his legs and untangled the umbilical cord. Now came the dangerous part. An infant's head was not made to be delivered after his torso. His chin would likely get hung up on the pelvic bones and push his head in a position that would make delivery nearly impossible. This dire possibility was what put the fear of God in Martha; in this moment, it was literally do or die.

What happened next startled Martha. She wondered if it was some sort of miracle, for she'd never seen anything like it. Just as her anxiety was spiking and she was about to start special maneuvers to deliver the baby's head, Marianne's pelvic bones opened like the gates of heaven for Saint Peter. The baby was delivered without the need for much intervention. The experience made Martha wonder what destiny awaited this anointed child.

Martha finally took a breath, unaware that she had been holding it unintentionally for the past minute or so. She got to work tying off and cutting the cord but then realized the baby was not crying. She glanced down at this new baby boy and quickly assessed that his color was improving, but without a cry. She knew he needed to have a nice loud cry to open his little lungs and get the amniotic fluid out. So she did what any experienced midwife would do in a situation like this: She held that babe up high by the ankles and gave him a good slap on the arse.

The infant's eyes opened wide and deviated toward her. His left hand fisted, flew out, and struck her right on the nose. Still no cry. Martha's eyes teared up from the blow, and she realized that the infant was now pink and breathing well but still not emitting a sound. She knew it was probably just the startle reflex that had prompted him to strike her, but the way he looked at her as he did it gave her pause. *This one has a bit of divil in him too*, she thought. She would ponder this moment throughout the rest of her career.

"Marianne, you have your first baby O'Neil! It's a boy!"

"You're wrong about that, *mo chara*.[2] He is not my *first* baby boy; he is THE O'Neil. I will never go through this again, that I promise you."

To that Martha had no reply. She dried off the babe and lifted him up to Marianne's breast to have his first feed, for which he seemed immensely grateful as he latched well and sucked vigorously. She delivered the placenta and checked the womb while the babe suckled.

Her job completed, Martha went out to tell John O'Neil the news and then to find a cool compress for her nose.

"Darling, we have a boy!" said John as he walked into the bedroom. "And he was born in Ireland, like we wanted." The couple had only recently returned to Ireland after both working for years in England.

"John, we have THE boy. I will not go through that ever again." Marianne was a strong woman, but the fear of her baby dying in childbirth was more than she could again contemplate enduring. "And John, *you* should not want to go through this again, either. "And as for his

---

[2] "My friend."

being born in Ireland, sure, it was the bittersweet mix of necessity, luck, and fate that brought us here."

Then they smiled at each other and said in perfect unison, as if practiced: "But mostly sweet."

John nodded silently, bent down, and kissed his wife's forehead. Then he pulled up a chair to watch his son continue to feed for the first time. He held the free hand of the love of his life and now mother of his son too. The three of them together, silent except for the sound of swallowing and an occasional slurp.

A NOVEL

The Baptism

The couple wanted to waste no time marking the official birth of their son. Marianne wanted to notify the Church right away and get him baptized. "John, first thing this morning I need you to go to the parish and get Father Mullarkey to set up his baptism and get his paperwork registered."

"Aye, that I will do. Let's get him recognized." Then he paused, his brow furled. "Just to be sure, so . . . what is it we will name him?"

"I want his middle name to be Torin because he will be a leader. A name is more than a label, it is a destiny."

"Aye, that's a good one." It was one of the names they had talked about, but it hadn't been definite until this moment. John wanted Marianne to have the final say on the matter of his name.

"I didn't finally decide on a first name until now. I pondered it overnight."

"Of course," John replied as he grabbed his hat and wedged it onto his head. The look on his face seemed to broadcast bated anticipation. His eyes squeezed halfway shut, and his mouth was drawn across his lower face in a geometrically straight line. He suspected what was coming.

"The."

"Thuh?"

"Not like thuh. Like Thee!" Marianne answered emphatically.

"Oh Jaysus, you know what Father Mullarkey would say to that, don't ya?" Now John was sweating as bad as Martha had been just a short time earlier.

"I don't give a damn about the Mullarkey of the Church," she exclaimed rather loudly while sending a piercing look to John.

John loved this woman for her strength, but sometimes that strength thrust him into uncomfortable situations, such as this one. He knew better than to respond. He just tucked his chin in anticipation of the soft Irish day outside the door, opened it, and took a determined step across the threshold.

A NOVEL

Mullarkey

"Hello, Father," John said as he entered the rectory, removing his cap with aplomb, swinging it across his body as he bent slightly at the waist.

"John, I hear congratulations are in order! A fine new baby boy has been added to our parish!"

"Aye, its's true. He's a scrapper too." John stepped around the wooden seat and sat facing the priest. "At least that's what Martha tells us."

"Well, knowing his parents, I can believe that." Father Mullarkey, smiling, leaned forward, propping himself up on his elbows. "So, I assume you're here to arrange the baptism."

"Aye."

"Well, let's get some information." He picked up the quill from the inkwell. "So, what's his name to be?"

"Torin, for a middle name."

"That's a good one! I don't think we have had a Torin in this parish!" The priest dipped his quill in ink and held it at the ready above the parchment below. "And what would be his first name?"

"The"

"The!"

"Yes, The."

Father Mullarkey's pen, unbeknownst to him, had vomited ink somehow all over the parchment in front of him. His face, beknown to him, had contorted into something that appeared demonic. "How dare you come to me with this joke!" he screamed.

"It's not a joke. That's what Marianne wants, and I agree. It is to be his first name."

"That is not a saint's name, and neither the Catholic Church nor I will have anything to do with it!" he yelled as he stood abruptly. "Get out!"

John knew that was the end of it. The only thing more immovable than Church dogma was his wife, Marianne. He was beset by difficulties with no good alternatives. He didn't care about Mullarkey's opinion, but he cared deeply for Marianne's. So, at least he knew where his heart lay.

Wedging his hat firmly onto his head, he turned and flung open the door. He expected once again to be greeted by the fine mist he had walked through on his way to the rectory. The bright daylight surprised him; the mist was nowhere to be felt. He slammed the door to make a point, causing dust to fall upon his shoulders.

The sudden sound startled a few doves, and they flew skyward into the now partly blue sky. His gaze drawn by the doves, he noticed the puffy clouds, and his childhood rushed back to him. He flashed back to those days when he had lain next to his da[3] on the dewy green grass, peering up at the sky as they took turns guessing the hidden pictures of clouds. He stopped walking, overcome by these bright and joyful memories. Just above him was a cloud shaped like the letter *X*. It slowly mutated into a letter *T* before finally deciding to turn into a cross and then dissipating into nothing. John chuckled as its meaning spoke to him. Then he said out loud in a whispered voice: "Aye, I see your meaning."

---

[3] His father.

A NOVEL

The Jesuit

"GET ME THE JESUIT!" she shouted so loudly that the dust that previously settled on the windowpane jumped off and flew for its life.

That was Marianne's reply, and it was just what John had expected, as evidenced by the fact he already had his hand on top of his hat to keep it from blowing off his head. He turned and went to complete his assigned mission.

The Jesuit was the closest thing the community had to a Druid priest. He followed a moral compass of what was right. He cared not about the laws of man nor those of the pope. For this reason, the Church didn't know what to do with him, so they made him a missionary of sorts to roam the countryside, willy-nilly, to spread the word of God to the barely Catholic population of County Wicklow. The pope feared that lately the Irish were tipping back to their pagan roots. Little did he know that the Jesuit was probably closer to Ireland's pagan roots than the parishioners were! And thus, he may have ended up sending more souls to righteousness than to the Church. He was happy to bend any rule. He performed baptisms near the clootie[4] tree at the spring. He forgave those who feared confession in the booth. He taught the outlawed Gaelic language—even though he himself didn't know much of it, but that wasn't really the point. He was what the local Irish people needed, and he needed them as well.

---

4   A **clootie well** is a holy well (or sacred spring), almost always with a tree growing beside it, where small strips of cloth or ribbons are left as part of a healing ritual, usually by tying them to branches of the tree (called a clootie tree, or rag tree). https://en.wikipedia.org/wiki/Holy_well

John tied an outlawed green ribbon on the clootie tree. That was the signal that the Jesuit required. Breaking the law was a risk, but anything worth doing had some risk. The Jesuit would then take the ribbon off and wander into town, knowing he would eventually find out who had left him this message. He would hide all the green ribbons underneath the floorboards in the confessional of Father Mullarkey's church because he thought that was funny. He had an Irish sense of humor, so.

The rap on the door had the Jesuit feel to it, so John happily opened the door. He knew that Marianne wouldn't rest until the paperwork was signed and filed.

"Father Bolger, welcome to our home."

"Glad to be here. I heard you needed to see me."

"Indeed we do," John replied as he opened the door wider and gestured for the Jesuit to come in.

Father Bolger entered, took off his cap, and sat down near the hearth. "So, what is it you need?"

"We need a baptism," replied Marianne as she entered the room and sat down intimidatingly close to the Jesuit.

"Well, that could be something that Mullarkey could do for you. Why me?"

"It's the babe's name that's the problem."

The Jesuit raised both eyebrows and asked, "Why is that a problem?"

"Because his name is to be The," John and Marianne replied in perfect harmony.

"The?"

"The."

"I see." The Jesuit rubbed his chin whiskers.

"Is that a problem for you?" Marianne's response was menacing.

The Jesuit guffawed with abandon. "Not for me. I love the name and am glad to be a part of your escapade."

"So, you'll do it?"

"Of course!" He gave Marianne a grand smile, his head swiveling right to left before replying. "Let's meet at daybreak tomorrow at the clootie tree."

At dawn the next day, the Jesuit gave The Torin O'Neil a "proper" baptism. After properly blessing the babe, he used the water from the spring. The certificate listed The's godparents as John's father and Marianne's mother—both deceased, but their presence there was felt by both John and Marianne. Since the couple had only recently returned to Ireland, in a county that was new to both, they did not have anyone they trusted enough to stand as godparents in this unorthodox baptism.

After the ceremony the Jesuit told John he would go straightaway to the church to slip the records into the parish files—no Mullarkey involved. On his way there, however, he had second thoughts. Knowing the current state of Ireland's political situation, he thought maybe *not* filing it might come in handy for this baby someday in the future. He decided right then he would not file it but just keep it safe. If the family later needed it filed, he could always do it then and make it seem as though he had forgotten.

At times during the ceremony, John had been overcome. He always was one to feel things more deeply than others, whether joy or sorrow. He had returned after many years to his home of Ireland. The famine had taken his entire family, yet here he was alive and with a family of his own. He had himself, so he did. He had Marianne. And now he had his son, The O'Neil.

THE O'NEIL

Weejon's Childhood

    John O'Neil, The O'Neil's father, was the youngest of four children of the O'Neil family, who were the proud owners of a small cottage on a tenant farm in County Roscommon, Ireland, in the shadow of the Kilronan Castle. It wasn't a shadow from the sun, as are most things. It was not close enough for that. It was the shadow of the landowner.

    The farm was a small plot of land full of rocky soil that had to be begged to grow anything other than potatoes. John knew from the time he could talk that there was not enough land to split between the four of them, so he always planned on leaving when he could, to set out on his own. He was lucky enough to be strong, independent, and intelligent. These qualities put the odds in his favor in the gambling casino of Ireland, where "the house" usually won it all.

    John's parents knew they could not afford more children, and this posed a challenge to them. They were too attracted to each other to keep their legs crossed, so they just had to keep their fingers crossed instead.

    When John was a baby, everyone referred to him as Wee John—first more clearly as Wee-Jon, but eventually the name melted into Weejon, and it stuck.

    Weejon started to read at age three years. His parents did not believe it at first, but by age five years, he was reading the few novels that they owned. He was especially interested in science and seemed obsessed to explore the surrounding fields for anything of interest. He understood the rocks and soil as if they were a part of him. He would spend time with anyone with any knowledge of the land's history or geology.

His da, Niall, was a coal miner at the Arigna fields. The name of the mine comes from an anglicization of the Gaelic word *An Airgnigh*, which meant "the plundering." It also was the name of the nearby river. The mine just borrowed it. It seemed a better name for the mine, though, as it was the mine owners who were indeed plundering its bounty.

It was a several-mile walk for Niall to get to the mine every day before sunrise. Coal had been taken from this particular mine since the Middle Ages, and it was famous for its shallow deposits. The miners would literally lie on their sides or back to scoop coal from the seams.

Weejon recalled his da swinging open the door upon returning home from work and exclaiming, "Bridget, what a great job I have! I get paid for lying on my back all day. Who else has a job like that?" To which Bridget, his love, would smirk and respond, "Well, I can think of one. And 'tis a job older than mining." They would have a good laugh over this, and sometimes Niall would reply, "Slaving for the rich, then, is the second oldest job since time began."

Weejon's first introduction into coal was from his da, who would bring chunks of coal or other interesting rocks home for his son to study. Weejon loved everything about rocks, and he researched any stones he received from his da. The one book that he most valued was a textbook on geology that his father had in his meager library. It had pictures and characteristics of any stones known to man at the time. In response to Weejon's enthusiasm, his da would smile and say to him, "Wee John, we are truly brethren of the stones."

When Weejon was old enough, Niall took him to the mines to work with him. He taught him everything he could about mining coal, the Earth, and Ireland. His da spoke of the land's political history as well as its geological history. Weejon, like a sponge, just soaked it all into his brilliant, hungry mind.

His favorite memories of childhood were the visits to his da at the mine. Niall arranged to meet with him for lunch whenever he could. They would eat together outside the mine, and afterward, if Nature cooperated, they would lie side by side and stare up at the clouds. They would try to find different shapes in the clouds and point them out to each other. One memorable day, Weejon asked, "Da, do you think the clouds are trying to tell us something by the shapes they take?"

A NOVEL

His da, silent for a minute before replying, replied, "They might be. Or it might just be yourself talking to yourself."

Weejon furrowed his brow briefly as he pondered his da's response, then nodded.

One day he asked about his nickname. "Da, why does everyone call me Weejon instead of John. John is my proper name, isn't it?"

"Yes, son, John is your proper name, but once a nickname gets placed, it's hard to remove."

"I think Weejon makes me sound like a baby."

"You're wrong there." Niall rolled to the side to face his son, a serious look upon his face. "Remember I told you about the Vikings' exploration and invasions into Ireland?"

"Aye."

"Well, that means that many of us here in Ireland carry some of that Viking blood. The blood of explorers and fighters. You may have some of that blood in you. So, think of your name as short for Norwegian. Then it becomes a strong name. Maybe that's where you got your red hair from."

From that day forward, Weejon wore his nickname with pride. It would be many years before he would again wished it to be changed.

Weejon's family had a plan for his siblings. Patrick, the eldest, already an apprentice miner, would inherit the cottage. He would be responsible for the house as well as for taking care of his parents in their old age. His sisters, Anne and Margaret, would, hopefully, marry and move into a small cottage of their own with their husbands. That was their plan, and it was the plan of many of the poor families around Ireland.

Weejon remembers a childhood filled with love and laughs. Their occasional hunger did not bother them, and it did not seem to inhibit Weejon's growth, for he grew into a formidable size even by twelve years of age.

The day that would stay cemented in his memory forever was the day that he left his loving family to travel to England to start his apprenticeship. After saying emotional goodbyes to his mother and siblings, he left the small cottage with his da. They had borrowed a horse cart to travel the twenty or so miles to the Sligo docks. From here "Weejon" (although everyone continued to call him by this moniker, he was anything but wee by then) would travel in steerage to his destination in England, the Ram Hill Colliery, for his apprenticeship.

The trip to Sligo went faster than he'd hoped, as he did not want to have to say goodbye to his da, but despite his wishes, the moment arrived. His da walked him to the ship and stood with him silently for a few minutes at the bottom of the ramp. After those few minutes, his da turned toward him, wrapped his arms around him, and held him as tightly as he could. With his lips near his son's ear, Niall whispered, "*Bi daingean agus fas i dtreo an tsolais.*"[5]

The words startled Weejon, as he'd never heard that saying before. He felt tears spilling down his cheeks. Niall then broke his grip, briefly looked his son in the eyes, man to man for the first time, then turned to walk back up the pier toward the road. He never looked back. Weejon watched him until he turned a corner and was out of sight. It was only then that he realized that his da had put something into his hand when he'd hugged him. He looked down, shocked, as if it had just materialized in his palm. He held it up and saw that it was a medallion on a leather lace. It was made of roughly hewn metal, obviously made with more heart than skill. It was just big enough to hold the words carved into its surface. He held it up in front of his eyes so he could read the carved letters. He read them out loud to himself: "*Bi daingean agus fas i dtreo an tsolais.*"

Tears flooded from his eyes as he tied the leather lace around his neck, vowing never to take it off. For he knew the meaning of these Gaelic words. He now repeated them out loud, this time in English: "Be strong and grow toward the light."

He had much time to think on this trip toward his new destiny in England. His childhood rushed through his thoughts, twisting his emotions like strands of wire. He grasped the medallion and smiled to himself. *This is my inheritance*, he thought. *That and the cost for my passage on this ship.*

---

5   "Be strong and grow toward the light."

He knew that the cost of this trip was likely more than his family could afford, but they had given it to him anyway. It was a *bon voyage* gift, a gift for a better future, but it was also a goodbye gift. He let go of the medallion just long enough to wipe another tear from his cheek. He grasped it again, his hand hugging it with the strength of a mother hugging her child. He held it in this way for as long as his hand could squeeze, but he eventually had to let go. The phrase carved on the medallion repeated in his thoughts. He did not know at that time that they were the last words that he would ever hear his da speak.

He thought about the Earth and its stones; they were to become his home, his past, and his future. He was bonded to them from an early age. He was now ready to start carving his own future. His da had got him apprenticed to a childless Irish family working at the Ram Hill Colliery in Bristol, England. Weejon was to learn as much as possible about mining coal, but he would have to do that on his own, without his family by his side. His only contact was to be the bittersweet letters he received from home. His family never broke their promise and wrote every month without fail.

THE O'NEIL

A NOVEL

Marianne's Childhood

Twelve-year-old Marianne, The O'Neil's future mother, stood at the bottom of the grand driveway, satchel in one hand and twirling a shamrock between her thumb and forefinger—the shamrock she had picked next to the entrance wall and the satchel that she had brought from the orphanage and that included the very few possessions she owned. She was about to enter the grounds of one of the wealthiest and grandest of mansions. This would be her home, really her job, for the next six years. Once she would turn eighteen, she hoped to go back to Ireland and forget England altogether.

The shamrock now captured her attention and directed her thoughts to her turbulent childhood. Marianne, you see, was even less lucky than most Irish children, who themselves never seemed to find the elusive luck of the Irish. When she was very young in the orphanage and was by herself, she would find a shamrock and pluck it. She would pretend that she was one leaf, and the other two leaves were her two sisters. She would bend the leaves toward each other as it they were whispering to each other, or she would press the leaves together like they were hugging. Her favorite game was spinning the shamrock back and forth between her thumb and forefinger like she was doing right now. She imagined that she was holding hands with her sisters and spinning around with them until they were all giddy with laughter and dizziness.

Now that she was older, the whole meaning of the shamrock had changed for Marianne. She realized that she was truly an orphaned only child and that the other two leaves, though they were indeed connected to her, represented poverty and hunger. She grunted as she thought, *Those are my actual sisters, and we three are all held together on a stem of English feudalism.*

She continued to ignore the beautiful mansion and grounds in front of her. Her thoughts remained trapped by the shamrock as it spun back and forth.

Before walking forward, Marianne allowed her mind to take one more look backward. When she'd reached nine years of age, she was told the story of her mother. On a day she had behaved particularly badly, the mother superior of the orphanage paddled her bum and then took her aside and told her the story. "Your mother was a beautiful and kind woman. She also was a good Catholic. She gave up her life so that you could live, much like Jesus gave his life for us." She patted Marianne and gave her a *tsk-tsk* as she shook her head. "So, you'd better make her sacrifice worth it."

Marianne found out about her father the following year, again after a day of particularly bad behavior. This story also came from the mother superior during a paddling episode. "Compared with your mother, your father was a loser. How she ended up with him is a mystery." She paused briefly and made a face that made Marianne think she was going to spit on the ground. "When your mother passed, it was only a matter of time before you came our way. He passed you off to neighbors and friends for a bit, but he knew that couldn't go on." Then she nodded gleefully, seeming happy to see him fail. "He was not a religious man, never came to church and never tithed, as was required." She again paused between paddling and chuckled out loud. "He left you right in the baby-go-round.[6] At least he had enough love left to give it a spin before he walked off. So that makes you the only donation he ever gave the church." She laughed loudly before continuing. "He rang the bell, walked away, and never turned back."

The mother superior loved to disparage Marianne's father from that day until the girl finally left the orphanage. Her experience at the orphanage had not been all bad, however. Even though the mother superior ran the place like a prison with an authoritarian iron fist, there were some nuns who had compassion and were more like big sisters than prison guards. It was those nuns who'd made survival possible, because who can survive without love and human interaction?

---

6   Boxes on a turntable mechanism that allow abandoned babies to be left in the church anonymously.

With that last thought, Marianne dropped the shamrock to the ground and with it the weight of her difficult life so far. She strode into the driveway with a gait suggesting she was a daughter of the mansion and not the new help. The only weight she carried on her shoulders was the weight of her linen dress straps.

The driveway drew her up toward the towering mansion and her future. Marianne told herself she would not look back, but she couldn't resist one last look over her shoulder at the mist rising from the stones.

This mansion was probably one of the best and biggest in all of England and certainly the best around Bristol. She continued her determined stride until she reached the large wooden door. Staring back at her was a large metal lion's head that served as the door knocker.

She reached up to grab it but then paused. She recalled the last words the mother superior had said to her before she left: "Don't you dare knock on the front door. That is for gentry, family, and valued guests. The *help* enters around the back. I warn you, Marianne, because I know you enough. You get that idea out of your head."

Knock! Knock! Two quick sharp loud knocks echoed into the mansion. Marianne put on the face of an innocent bog-hopper (she had practiced that look just for this occasion) and waited.

The door swung open gently, and a formally dressed butler peered out over her head, his snout elevated as if about to sniff the wind. He slowly bent his neck down toward Marianne. His eyes widened, and he then really did sniff.

"Good day, good sir," Marianne said and fluttered her eyes. "I am Marianne, the new maid."

The butler nearly fell over when he stepped back in preparation to slam the door in her face as he said, "Don't you dare ever knock on this front door again! Help goes around the back!" With that said, he did slam the door in her face. The force seemed to waken the sleeping lion door knocker, which raised abruptly and fell back into the door with another loud knock. Marianne smiled and thanked the lion. She preferred things in threes. She hoped the pompous butler heard the knock and would think it was from her.

As she walked around the side of the house, her thoughts now passed to what little she knew about the home she would be both serving and living in for the next six years of her life. She knew it had been stolen from an Irish Catholic family and bequeathed to an Irish Protestant who'd helped subdue her own people a very long time before. This upset her, as she knew she would once again have to bend a knee to these vultures.

As she approached the back door to give it a knock, she broke out in a belly laugh. *I guess this place, then, is more of a "Mick" mansion than just a mansion.*

The door opened, and a middle-aged woman in a maid's outfit said, "Jaysus, girl, whatever is so funny?" Her accent definitely came from Ireland but not from a county Marianne could accurately place—maybe County Cork?

"Just thinking about history," Marianne replied as she sashayed through the door. "Always seem to find fun in that."

"Well, I am dying of curiosity, so please tell."

Marianne, whether out of overconfidence or just immediately trusting this person, told her the story of the front door and her thoughts about the "Mick" mansion. She also told her that she had strict instructions to never knock on the front door but did it anyway, acting all innocent and stupid.

"That must have been Gillies, the butler. His head is so far up the lord's arse I am surprised he even heard you knock."

"He did seem a bit haughty," Marianne replied as she looked around at her new surroundings.

"Well, lassie, I think we are going to be good friends! My name is Sophie—at least that is what everyone here calls me. I prefer Sadhbh,[7] my Gaelic name." She reached out and grasped Marianne's two hands in hers. "The name is illegal to use here or in Ireland, as the Gaelic has been outlawed, but I don't give a rat's arse for that."

---

[7] Pronounced "Sigh-ve."

To that answer Marianne smiled broadly and thought, *Maybe with Sadhbh here, this situation won't be so bad. I wish I'd had a Sadhbh at the orphanage.*

"Let me show you around and where you will sleep," Sadhbh offered.

Marianne slung her bag of meager belongings over her shoulder and followed Sadhbh out of the room.

THE O'NEIL

Weejon's Work Life

Weejon came off the ship, anxious but hopeful. He walked down the plank, his eyes darting left and right, hoping someone was there for him in this strange country.

"Oy, Weejon! Over here."

Weejon looked in the direction of the alert and saw the smiling face of a thin man with flaming red hair who was waving frantically. The man's smile made it seem as though he had just won the best pig competition at the county fair. Weejon would soon realize that that smile almost never faded, no matter what the weather.

Weejon headed in the man's direction and was soon startled to be wrapped in a bear hug. Already at age twelve, Weejon towered over the man, but he was amazed by how safe that hug made him feel. He immediately relaxed.

"My name is Mr. Gara, Weejon," the man said as he looked pensively toward the clouds. "Well, that's what everyone calls me. Even my wife calls me that." His smile widened at the mention of his wife, and a chuckle escaped. "In fact, it has been so long that anyone used my first name, I am not sure I could tell you what it is for a hundred pounds!"

On the trip back to the Gara cottage, Mr. Gara told the story of his best childhood friend, Niall, Weejon's da. He told Weejon that Niall was not only his best friend but the best human he ever knew. He followed this by telling about some of the misadventures that neither one of them were proud of but nonetheless made both laugh hysterically.

As they arrived at the meager, broken-down home of the Garas, Weejon wondered how it still stood against the storms and wind. Once he entered, though, he immediately knew the answer to his wonderment. He felt an overwhelming love that he could not explain. He had always been deeply loved by his parents, a love he never doubted. It seemed as though here was an even higher love, something he had not known existed. This love was something entirely new and mystical. Weejon seemed to lose his breath. This love was a force that held up the walls better than any wooden beams could.

"*Mo gra*,[8] I have Weejon!"

Mrs. Gara appeared magically in front of them and darted toward Weejon, startling him with her suddenness. Without a word, she wrapped her arms around him in another warm embrace, which competed with her husband's for the best embrace ever. Weejon teared up and sniffled. "Hello, Weejon," she said. "Welcome to our home."

Mr. Gara, seeing Weejon's tears, said, "Don't feel bad about the tears. Mo gra is a powerful force, and although she will not hug many, those she does hug experience the same result."

They showed Weejon his room, which they had prepared from their living room. When Weejon protested, they insisted that the only time they spend awake in the home is either in the kitchen or, if weather permitted, in the garden. They told him the arrangement was no trouble.

Weejon noticed over the next few days that "the garden" they referred to was nothing but a rock garden. He was sure they couldn't even get a potato to grow there without a few Hail Marys and a blessing by the bishop. The situation reminded him of his parents' home, and he wondered how the couple survived here on Mr. Gara's mining salary, which he knew from his da's job was barely subsistence wages. Yet here they were, both as thin as he thought possible but as happy as he ever knew two humans to be. Obviously, their riches lay not in quids and coins but in love and laughter.

Weejon settled into a pattern of daily work with Mr. Gara. They woke early in order to get to the mine by seven a.m. The three-mile walk to

---

8 "My love."

the Ram Hill Colliery was fine in good weather or on soft days but not so good on those days that were not so soft.

Mrs. Gara always had breakfast for them—that is, when she had food. Sometimes hardtack bread was the best she could find. She could not prepare lunch for then if she had nothing to give. On those days she still gave them a lunch box, though. When the pair got to their lunch break, they would look at each other, smile, and open the lunch box with anticipation. On the days she had no food to prepare, she had left them a little note. Sometimes a poem. Weejon's note was usually something about how much she loved him. Well, that's what his note said, but from the look on Mr. Gara's face, it seemed *his* might have been even better! The notes somehow, mysteriously, sated them both. Weejon got to a point where no matter how hungry he was, he preferred his note to food.

Weejon's stomach rumbled loudly at times, but the love of this home was so loud he never heard it. The next six years would be when he learned mining, the love of others, and more importantly truths about himself. He learned to be happy and comfortable in his own shoes, even if those shoes had holes in them. He knew that Mr. and Mrs. Gara loved him and that they kept him safe, but they also let him be himself and let him make mistakes. It was the mistakes that taught him more than anything, both about himself and about the world around him.

The couple had a sense of humor that kept Weejon laughing, as the following story illustrates:

Many nights when they came home, Mrs. Gara would be silently knitting in her rocking chair. Mr. Gara would occasionally ask, "*Mo gra*, what are you making? You've been working on that thing for weeks now."

"Never you mind," she firmly replied while continuing to rock. "You will find out soon enough!"

From the tone of his wife's voice, Mr. Gara knew to be silent and to change the subject. As the three conversed by the fire, the knitting continued for many nights.

One special night when the pair arrived back from the mine, they immediately noticed the smile across Mrs. Gara's face. "Well," remarked Mr. Gara, "you look like you just ate the last piece of rhubarb pie!"

"Come in here," she said as she turned and stepped back from the door. "I have a present for both of ye."

Weejon looked at Mr. Gara and shrugged; then he followed him through the door.

Mrs. Gara reached down to the chair and lifted a piece of folded knitted cloth. She turned back toward them. "I made a special blanket for each of you."

"So that's what you have been working on all this time." Mr. Gara smiled toward the love of his life.

With that she dramatically flicked the cloth open, holding it up in front of her to display to the pair what she had made.

"Why," exclaimed a puzzled Mr. Gara, glancing toward Weejon, "that blanket seems to have arms on it!"

"That's what makes it so special!" She tried to hold in a laugh. "It's a blanket that walks around with you."

"I'll be damned! That's amazing! I never heard of such a thing." Mr. Gara started to laugh. "We could change the world with this thing!"

Weejon was a bit confused at first, for to him the thing looked like a sweater. He wasn't sure what was going on until Mr. Gara put on his "blanket." Then he got the joke.

"Look at me, *mo gra*!" Mr. Gara announced while he paraded around the small home like a peacock. "It really works! It's staying with me as I walk."

Mrs. Gara turned to Weejon. "Weejon, try yours on."

Weejon put on his "blanket with the arms" and joined Mr. Gara, and they paraded around the room like two fools. They jumped and spun and pranced, and sure enough, that blanket stayed right with them. Then the three of them nearly fell to the floor laughing.

Many nights the trio sat in front of the small fireplace and talked, or they just silently sat together. The excitement, at least for Weejon, was getting a letter from his parents. One would arrive every month without fail. Weejon, who had been taught reading by his parents as well as by a local Jesuit, would read them aloud. Some nights, if Weejon was feeling homesick, Mrs. Gara would read them for him. Weejon noticed that on some nights, Mr. Gara would have an unusual look on his face; his smile seemed to be only half-hearted. Weejon remembered one night particularly well: "*Mo gra*," his wife said, "you look like you just swallowed sour milk. What's wrong.?"

Mr. Gara turned red as a beet, for he'd never spoken of this with his wife. He stammered and shifted in his chair. "When you read these letters, it makes me think how good it would be to know how to read. I guess I just feel bad that I don't know how to read. I looked at those letters, and they only look like scribble to me." He stared at the floor, a bit embarrassed that he had brought the subject up. "I am sorry for feeling sorry for myself. I should not have said anything."

Weejon turned to Mrs. Gara. He felt pinpricks in his face. Why had he not seen the obvious? It was evident from her blushing face that Mrs. Gara must be feeling a guilt similar to his. "*Mo gra*," she said softly, "I never knew you wanted to learn to read."

"Well, hmm . . . well, you know . . . hmm . . . I was just thinking out loud."

Weejon and Mrs. Gara faced each other; he winked and she offered a barely perceptible nod. They now knew what they were going to do. She looked her husband right in the eye. "Well, it would be no trouble for us to teach you." She turned back to their young boarder. "Right, Weejon?"

"I would be honored! It would be like paying you back for teaching me about coal mining."

"Well, if it wouldn't be too much trouble," Mr. Gara replied quietly, looking down at his feet.

"So, it's set." Mrs. Gara got to her feet. "Weejon and I will take turns teaching you the written word!" She fetched the kettle and put it on the stove. "It will be another adventure for us, mo gra."

The trio settled into a pattern: Six days a week there was work, but at night they worked by candlelight (when they had candles) or by spelling bees in the dark, all to teach Mr. Gara how to read. It soon became apparent that he did not have a natural talent for the written word, but Mrs. Gara and Weejon were undaunted, and Mr. Gara was indefatigable.

The ensuing six years for Weejon were filled with hunger and homesickness, but the love of the Garas overcame those feelings. He realized that with love nothing else really mattered.

As Weejon approached his eighteenth birthday and started to stress about what he would do next, he had an idea. Mr. Gara had finally figured out reading, and he was as pleased as punch. Reading gave him a confidence and pride beyond his skill with mining coal, a confidence and pride that his two housemates felt in every word he spoke. Weejon had heard of the book *Rob Roy* by Walter Scott, which he felt Mr. Gara would appreciate, since the Scots and the Irish had both a common ancestry as well as a common historical struggle. He resolved to get this book, somehow, and to give it to Mr. Gara as a parting gift. He knew of a bookstore in Bristol, but then there was the issue of money. He had to figure out a way to get enough money to buy his host this book before he left.

Weejon started to take walks by himself whenever he could. The summer months provided many hours of sunshine after work hours, and he was able to break free for a few hours on Sundays after the family meal. He confided with Mrs. Gara because he needed her to cover for him. Instead of walking, he would pick up odd jobs for a small payment, which he stowed away until he had enough for the gift. He loved to work, but these little jobs gave him even more joy than working side by side with Mr. Gara in the mine, for he knew they would end with a gift for Mr. Gara. Eventually, he had saved enough to buy the book. The next step was to get to Bristol, which was more than a few miles away. He just hoped that the bookstore had the book he wanted.

Marianne's Work Life

Marianne settled into her role as a "utility" maid. Her main job was cleaning, but she quickly learned that she was required to fill in for any other job needed at the time. She would clean but also help in the kitchen, help with the laundry, serve food dinners, and even work in the garden. She grew closer to Sadhbh, who kept a watchful eye out for her.

She felt free in some ways, certainly freer than she had been in the orphanage. She thought of herself as air because that's how the lord and the lady treated all of the help. The servants were invisible to them but necessary to run the manor. Marianne always grinned when they received no recognition for the work they did. It was as if plates of food appeared magically in front of the lord and lady. Some of the servants took offense to being completely ignored, but Marianne thought it was just fine. She had no desire to make any connection with these arrogant rich Brits.

Marianne was on the floor of her room on all fours when Sadhbh suddenly walked in. "What are you doing down on the floor?"

Marianne jumped up startled but immediately felt relief when she saw it was Sadhbh. "Come here, and I will show you." She lifted one of the loose floorboards, pulled out a book, and held it up for Sadhbh to see.

"Jane Austen," Sadhbh said. "Wow, that's a good one! I didn't know that you could read. I can't imagine that the nuns would have taught you."

Marianne scrunched up her face. "No way! The nuns only taught us that we should be subservient to God, nuns, and men, in that order." She shrugged her shoulders with her arms extended in jest. "Why would we need to read?"

"Well now," Sadhbh said as she sat on the bed, "I am curious to find out this story."

"There was a traveling Jesuit who wandered the countryside, looking for lost souls to save. He came by every week to teach us to read and write. He even taught us some mathematics." She smiled, and her eyes drifted away momentarily as she recalled those rare good memories of the orphanage. "The nuns were furious, but they really couldn't do a thing about it. He really didn't care what they thought." She sat down on the floor, and Sadhbh sidled up next to her, both of them facing the books. "And we considered it a fantastic way to get some revenge on the nuns."

"Well, it seems as though you learned to not only read but how to be a rebel!" Sadhbh's arms were akimbo in a fake (teasing) scolding posture. "So, I guess it is the rebel in you that decided to steal books from the lord's library, then."

"Borrow, not steal. The library is huge, and I have never seen either of them read anything but the financial or society page in the newspaper. I didn't think they would mind." The two leaned into each other, both giggling. "And by that, I mean they would not know I was reading them."

Sadhbh picked up the book and looked again at the cover. "Jane Austen's *Pride and Prejudice*—you picked a good one here."

"Have you read it?"

"Of course." She winked. "I have the same library card as you!"

And with that they both had a hearty laugh and then shared their opinions of different books that they had read.

"There is one type of book you won't find in their library, though," Sadhbh cautioned. "Any book written by an Irishman or any book that could be construed as supporting the Irish or Scottish causes. Those books are banned." She contracted her face into a grimace. "Such a book might give people the wrong ideas about who should be in charge."

Marianne nodded. She was sure that she would like to read some of those books.

Sadhbh then gently held Marianne's hand and spoke in a hushed, serious tone. "I need to ask you something."

Marianne focused on Sadhbh's face with intense curiosity and waited silently.

"Now that you have been here for a while and I feel I know you well, I wanted to ask if you want to join me in a little business that I have running behind the scenes."

"Of course, I would like to help you any way I can."

Sadhbh then explained that she had a little side business of laundering and sewing and sometimes cleaning. "The local merchants and people of modest means will leave clothing for wash or something that needs repairs in the bushes down near the manor gate. When they put something there, they leave a rock on top of the wall, so I know there is something there to pick up. I will then just add it in to the wash being done here and sort it out later. Or if it is sewing that's needed, I will do that." She had a look of pride on her face as she revealed her cunning plan. "It looks like I am just tending to the lord and lady, so no one is any the wiser." The look of pride changed to a smile. "I leave the completed work back where I found it and place two rocks on the wall. When the customer picks up the work, they take the rocks off and leave a few pence on the wall."

Marianne could barely contain her excitement. This "little side business" would give her a chance to save money for passage back to Ireland! Here she was only paid in the food she ate and the bed she slept in. When new clothing was needed, the lord and lady would provide that, but they paid no wages. So, in reality she had no money of her own. The lord and lady liked it that way, as it kept the help trapped right there in their mansion. "I will join you!"

And with that they shook hands, and their business partnership began. Ireland seemed closer with every coin Marianne added to her stash under the floorboards.

THE O'NEIL

A NOVEL

The Bookstore

Marianne wanted to get a gift for Sadhbh, and she knew just what it should be. She knew that Sir Walter Scott had written a book called *Rob Roy*. She knew it was about the Jacobite rebellion in Scotland in the 1700s. She had not read it, but she was certain it was rebellious enough that it would never be found in "their library."

Marianne had purchased some nice clothes to wear on her unauthorized excursions into Bristol. The clothes served as a disguise, of course, but they also made her safer. The riffraff would not bother a lady of means. The help sometimes had free time on Sunday, but the stores in town were closed then, so Sunday would not work. She would have to slip away during the week. Sadhbh would cover for her, just as Marianne covered for Sadhbh whenever her friend needed it.

Marianne purchased *Rob Roy* from the merchant but stayed a while longer to browse all the other wonderful books. She was near the back of the store when she heard the front doorbell tinkle. She reflexively looked toward the direction of the sound, and that's when she first laid eyes on him. The sight took her breath away. She stared. He was tall, with curly red hair, and he had strong muscular arms. It was the arms that trapped her stare. Not only were they muscular; they were glistening and deeply tanned. They looked like they had been chiseled out of iron. The man was covered in coal dust from head to toe. At that moment Marianne felt in her core just what Jane Austen's controversial stories were depicting.

She eavesdropped on their conversation.

"Hello, kind sir," the man said as he removed his dusty cap. "I am looking for a book."

The merchant regarded the man as though he were a foreign invader, one who definitely did not belong in his shop. He answered sarcastically: "Well, you must be a genius! This *is* a bookstore, you know."

Weejon stuttered and grabbed at the collar of his shirt, which suddenly felt a little too tight. "What I meant is that I want a particular book."

"Come on, man, get to it so you can get out of my shop with your filthy clothes."

"I am looking for a book called *Rob Roy*. Have you heard of it?"

"Of course, I've heard of it, you *eejit*!"[9] The merchant slammed his hands down on the counter for emphasis. "But you are out of luck because I just sold the last copy to that woman over there." He gestured toward the back of the store.

Weejon was crestfallen. He'd had his heart set on getting Mr. Gara that book. He froze there because he really did not have another plan. And that's when he heard a soft voice behind him: "I couldn't help but overhear that you wanted this book."

Weejon turned around, and he saw the most beautiful woman he'd ever laid eyes on. She was dressed in expensive clothes, so she must be a lady of some means. Why would she even acknowledge him? She was holding the very book, *Rob Roy*, up toward him.

"Yes, I did seek to buy that book." His collar tightened even more. He was embarrassed. How must he appear to this fancy woman?

"Well, if you can explain to me why you wanted this book, and if your reason is better than mine, I might consider selling it to you."

Weejon started to speak, but Marianne hushed him: "Not here. I would prefer to talk over tea."

Weejon knew he just had enough to buy the book and if he now had to pay for tea, he would not have enough left to buy the book. Being an honest and direct man, he told her this outright.

---

9 "You idiot!"

Marianne, impressed by his honesty, replied, "Don't worry about that. We can work something out." She then slipped her arm around his and led him out the door. Her nice clean clothes immediately picked up a coating of coal dust anywhere she contacted him.

She led him to a small tea shop nearby, and they sat down. She ordered tea and biscuits for them. Weejon was secretly adding up the cost and comparing it to what was in his pocket. He knew that he had to insist that he pay, even though she was obviously better off financially than he.

"Let's start with our names," Marianne started the conversation. "I am Marianne Donegan."

"I am Wee—...uh...I am John O'Neil." He was surprised that for the first time in a long while he felt embarrassed to use his nickname. He told her about the Garas and his gift idea for Mr. Gara. He told her about his childhood and about his separation from his family back in Ireland.

Sitting this close to him, Marianne could barely keep from jumping over the table and kissing him, but she kept a calm, external look. "Well, that is a very noble gift and a wonderful story." She reached out to touch the book on the table, purposefully brushing against Weejon's hand. "Now it is my turn to tell you my story. I think you will be surprised."

Weejon shifted in his chair and leaned forward, both in anticipation and in just getting as close as he could to this beautiful woman. He was in a dream, and he was afraid to wake up from it.

She told him everything: from her upbringing in the orphanage, about her current job, about Sadhbh and the banned books. She told him about the business that they ran to earn their own money. And she told him about her disguise. The more she said, the more she could see him relax.

Weejon was smiling as he realized she was not in a class above him. He also allowed his mind to imagine that he was going to marry this woman. "Your disguise is very good. You had me fooled. Dressed as I am, I couldn't imagine why such a beautiful woman would even see me, not to mention talk to me."

They both laughed. Then Marianne reached across the table and held his hand. Weejon's heart rate shot up when she squeezed his hand firmly and said, "I think your story beats mine, so I think you get the book." With her side business, Marianne could earn enough to give Sadhbh a different book, since this was the only copy of Rob Roy available; she had seen several other "banned" books on the bookstore's shelves.

Weejon, having paid for the tea and biscuits, did not have enough left to buy the book from Marianne. "But I cannot buy the book from you after paying for the tea and biscuits."

"That's exactly what I wanted to happen." Her sly response, delivered with a slightly roguish smile, puzzled Weejon, and he squinted his eyes. "I think we will need to arrange a payment plan for you. Let me think." She tapped her finger against the side of her head in feigned deep concentration. "What would be a fair arrangement?" Her finger stopped tapping and jolted from her head, pointing upward. "I know. You must meet me here every week to have tea with me."

Weejon almost let out a scream. This was the best business arrangement ever offered to anyone. He was going to see her again! *It's not a dream.* He was in love, and he knew they would marry someday and return to Ireland. He just knew. "I will meet you here every week or die trying, I promise."

She handed the book across the table. "Well then, John. I look forward to seeing you again."

As Marianne disappeared around the corner of the shop, Weejon broke into a run fueled by excitement. Not only did he have the book for Mr. Gara, he had just met the most wonderful woman! The miles passed quickly, and soon he burst through the door of the Garas' cottage, calling out their names.

He stood in front of the couple, hiding the book behind him. A puzzled look was on Mr. Gara's face, but a knowing look was on Mrs. Gara's. "I have a surprise for you, Mr. Gara." He pulled the book from behind his back.

Mr. Gara trembled but was silent. He took the book into his hands and turned his head down toward it. Tears began spilling down his cheeks. Almost silently he wept. Once he'd regained his composure, he gazed at both his housemates. In a choking voice he simply said, "This is the first book I ever owned."

The three then retired to sit in front of their meager fireplace in the room full of their meager belongings, and once again their shared love filled the air.

Mrs. Gara told her husband about how she and Weejon had executed the plan and about the side money Weejon had been earning to afford the book. Weejon excitedly told his hosts about his trip to the bookstore and about spending time with the most wonderful woman he'd ever met. They could see he was already in love.

Mr. Gara then read out loud from his new book, and Mrs. Gara and Weejon happily listened as the story of the previous century's Scotland in turmoil began to unfold from his slowly spoken words. The three of them continued this way for quite some time that night.

THE O'NEIL

A NOVEL

The Famine

Weejon heard about the famine in a locust swarm of newsprint as it flew over the Irish Sea to England. This plague invaded his mind and fed his anxieties. He waited anxiously for his next letter from home.

As he walked through the English country fields, he paid particular attention to the homes and the people around him. He looked for any signs of famine here, but he could find none. He tried his best to reassure himself: "Surely things cannot be that bad in Ireland when things look fine here," he mumbled to himself. "Surely, the English would not allow their own subjects to starve."

His mind was so restless, he paced around the outside of the Garas' cottage now more than ever before. Alone with his thoughts. The Garas tried their best to give him comfort, but a letter from his parents would be the only remedy. Weejon certainly appreciated everything they had been doing for him both now and in the past, but he just could not get rid of this feeling of dread.

When the letter from home was a week late, he became apoplectic. If it hadn't been for Marianne, he would not have been able to function normally. It was during this period that his closeness to her grew exponentially. Her soul filled his heart, and he felt as though his heart filled her soul. They continued to meet weekly at the tea shop, and this became Weejon's lifeline during this difficult time. They took turns paying the bill now, as they both had streams of income; Weejon's came from his continued odd jobs, and Marianne's from her side business. They promised each other to save as much as they could so that someday they could return to Ireland together.

"A letter from home is now over two months late," Weejon stated with a trembling voice. "I should have received at least two letters by now."

Marianne reached across the table to grasp both of his hands. "Oh John"—she never used his nickname—"we will get through this together, no matter what the outcome. I will always be by your side."

"I don't know what I would do without you and the Garas. Especially now."

"Let's talk about our future together when we return to Ireland. It gives me such joy to think about that. Maybe it will give you some comfort, even if only for a little while."

"Aye" is all he replied as his mind swirled.

Marianne knew in her bones that bad news was coming, and she knew it would come like a storm from the western sea. She hoped it would not be as devastating as she expected. She hoped that she could be his life ring when the tidal wave came to shore.

And that wave did strike indeed, with the force of a gale. It came not in rain and floods but in the form of a telegram. The knock on the door in the middle of the day startled Mrs. Gara. They rarely had visitors, at least never unexpected ones.

She opened the door to find a young messenger boy, hat in hand with a Cockney accent on his tongue. "G'day, ma'am. Telegram for . . ."—he glanced down at the envelope—"for the Garas."

She reached out for the envelope but had trouble grasping it as her hand was shaking violently. "Thank you, young man," she replied. Then she continued: "Let me give you something for your trouble."

"No need for that, ma'am," he answered as he looked around at the small cottage, realizing that this woman lived in a poverty similar to the one in which he had been born.

"Nonsense, I insist."

Mrs. Gara had not a shilling to spare, but she had just made fresh damson and honey scones. She'd had enough ingredients to make only three, one for each of them, but she now decided she would give hers to this young lad. He appeared hungry. For Mrs. Gara, love and kindness seemed to fill her up more than any food ever could.

"Thank you, ma'am. That is very kind." He took the still warm scone into his hand. His mouth watered and his stomach rumbled in unrecognized thanks as well.

Once the door closed, he placed his hat back on, turned, and walked back to the road. He devoured the scone as soon as he was out of sight of the cottage. He said aloud, "That was the best damn scone I ever tasted."

Meanwhile, Mrs. Gara sat frozen in her chair near the fireplace, hand folded over the envelope in her lap. She did not move the rest of the afternoon. She seemed to already know what the telegram was going to say. She just couldn't be sure how bad.

"*Mo gra*, we're home," Mr. Gara announced as he stepped over the threshold. Then he held his breath. His heart seemed to miss a few beats. He could feel something deep in his soul. Something dreadful.

"Come sit, my loves."

Mr. Gara and Weejon glanced at each other as they stepped toward the fireplace and took their seats.

"You received a telegram, Weejon," she stated as she looked tearfully at them both.

"A telegram from whom?"

"It's from a Father Duffy."

"I don't know that name. What does it say?"

"That's all I know. I didn't read it. I wanted to wait for you to come home."

Weejon, of course, realized what the news was in this telegram, so he said, "Will you read it to me? I don't think I will be able to get through it." Tears began spilling down his cheeks.

Mrs. Gara opened the envelope and began:

> *IT IS WITH GREAT SADNESS THAT I INFORM YOU OF THE TRAGIC DEATH OF YOUR PARENTS AND REMAINING SIBLINGS STOP THE FAMINE TOOK THEM BACK TO THEIR CREATOR STOP MAY THE LORD AND SAVIOUR JESUS CHRIST COMFORT YOU DURING THIS DARK TIME STOP FATHER DUFFY END*

Silence filled the room as she finished reading. The silence lasted seconds, but it seemed like hours. Then Mr. and Mrs. Gara, both crying, rose from their chairs and rushed to Weejon. They both wrapped their arms around him and stayed that way for a long time, all three of them sobbing deeply and loudly.

Weejon eventually stopped sobbing enough to say, "I have to go see Marianne."

They stopped embracing as all three stood, trying to wipe away tears that felt as though they would never stop.

"I love you," Weejon said as he grabbed his cap and turned toward the door.

Mr. and Mrs. Gara both stood on the front step and watched Weejon run across the fields as he had done so many times before on much happier days. They did notice that he'd never run as fast as he did that day.

Weejon arrived at the back door of the mansion for the first time. He knocked hesitantly, as he was not sure what kind of trouble his visit might cause for Marianne.

The door opened to reveal Sadhbh holding a rag. She had not met Weejon, but she knew all about him from Marianne. He stood there, covered in coal dust that had been turned to mud by sweat, tears, and the soft rain falling. His face was flushed, and he was gasping for air. Sadhbh could see a broken man in front of her.

"I need to see Marianne," he said once he had enough breath to speak.

"Come in." She led him to a seat at the table and placed a freshly brewed cup of tea in front of him. "I will get her."

Marianne arrived in the kitchen a few minutes later. Her surprise quickly turned to dread once she saw him. "Oh, John, you received news."

"Marianne, they are all gone. The famine took them all."

Marianne ran to him, spilling both tea and cup to the floor as she kissed him firmly on his lips and held that kiss for a very long time. A kiss that tasted like salty tears and coal. She did not want to break away from this kiss, as she hoped she could draw some of his sadness away into her to lessen his burden.

"What am I to do now? I always thought I would return to Ireland to be near them once I finished in England. Where do I go now?"

"You have me and always will. Weejon"—it was the only time she used his nickname—"we will find a new home in Ireland together and raise a family."

There it was. The proposal that they both wanted. The loss of his family made it more real. He was adrift, and he knew only this woman could keep him from drowning.

"I love you intensely, Marianne," he replied firmly and then gave her another very long kiss.

THE O'NEIL

The Marriage

Weejon's heart was broken, and he would have remained a broken man if it hadn't been for the support of the Garas and Marianne. Marianne arranged for Sadhbh to cover for her so she could spend more time with Weejon. She knew the only way to stitch a broken heart back together was through sutures made of love. She had plenty to give him, and the Garas helped.

Mr. Gara borrowed a donkey cart from a neighbor so Weejon could visit Marianne every evening. It saved the time that walking would have cost.

"It was nice of the Mulgrews to lend you their cart," stated Mrs. Gara.

"Yes, they are gems, those Mulgrews."

"I hope you offered something in return." Mrs. Gara squinted at her husband.

"Of course! I am not an *eejit*! They tried to refuse, knowing we don't have any money to spare, but I insisted," replied Mr. Gara, taking a few steps back away from his wife. His face formed a sheepish grin, overlaid with some anticipation of what was to come.

"I don't much like the look on your face right now,"

"I told them that you would love to bake them a whole dozen of those wonderful scones of yours."

Mrs. Gara replied with a swift swat to his bum with the rug beater she was holding. The few steps he had taken backward did not save him from her wrath. "Oh, you are the most generous soul in all of England when it comes to volunteering someone else slaving over a hot stove."

Then she ran toward him and raised the rug beater again. He anticipated her move and was already running around the cottage. She gave chase round and round. In between gasping breaths, he yelled out as he ran, "You won't ... believe what ... the donkey is called ... Cupid!"

Mrs. Gara stopped in her tracks by this news and started to chuckle. The chuckle slowly grew into hysterics. They both fell to the ground and enjoyed a good laugh together.

Once Mrs. Gara caught her breath as her laughing slowed, she just added one more thing: "You're still an *eejit!*"

Marianne poured as much love as she could into Weejon, and gradually he felt that his heart was starting to beat again. The next few weeks saw them growing closer than ever. They were deeply in love.

"Marianne, we need to plan our future." He took her hands and intertwined his fingers with hers. "I know only two things. I want to spend the rest of my life with you, and I want to spend that life in Ireland."

"Then we have the exact same plan. I love you, John," she replied as she squeezed his hand even tighter.

During many of their nights together, they spoke of their plans. Marianne had saved sufficient funds over the years for passage to Ireland for them both. They would need more than that, though, in order to start a life together.

Weejon had saved some meager funds, but he really wanted to give it to the Garas when it was time to leave. He felt so indebted to them for everything they did for him. The only possessions he owned were his mining tools, which took much of his money, and the medallion his da had given him when he left Ireland. He wore that medallion every day, and now its value was beyond priceless to him. It was now the only thing he had left to remember his parents by. As long as he lived, he would never take it off.

A NOVEL

The couple were really in a bind. They had no idea where to lay down roots now that County Roscommon had been taken away from Weejon.

The Garas, however, did have a plan, and they were about to put it into action. "Weejon," Mr. Gara said as he laid his hand on Weejon's shoulder, "we want you to invite Marianne to come for dinner on Sunday." He glanced at his wife, and she nodded back to reinforce what he was saying. "It has been some time since we have seen her, and with your time here getting short, we really want to spend some time with her."

"I know she would love to see you."

With that the Garas again glanced slyly at each other and gave a wink, which Weejon missed.

Sunday came, and Weejon was excited. He and Marianne had a big surprise for the Garas, and he was about to burst if he had to hold the news in any longer.

Mrs. Gara prepared one of the best meals she had ever made. She somehow got hold of some ham, and she also made one of Marianne's favorite, colcannon! There was plenty of both too.

In the center of the table was what looked to Weejon to be a bottle of poteen. This surprised him because he'd never seen either of the Garas drink alcohol. He pointed to the bottle. "Is that poteen?"

"It is indeed," replied Mrs. Gara. "It is part of the surprise we have for you."

Puzzled, Marianne looked at Weejon and just shrugged.

"Let's finish eating," Mrs. Gara said, "and then we will all raise a glass." She looked right into the eyes of the couple across the table. "Who knows? Maybe there will be a toast in order."

Weejon had always thought that Mrs. Gara might be fey, but tonight he knew it for sure. *They already know what our surprise is, and they even set us up with this nice meal.*

After the meal, as they retired around the fireplace, leaving dishes where they lay, Mrs. Gara passed out some glasses. Mr. Gara used his teeth to pull out the cork from the bottle and proceeded to fill everyone's glass.

Once they each had a full glass, Weejon suddenly let out a gasp. He was reacting to Marianne's elbow striking him in his ribs. He turned reflexively toward her and saw her eyes open wide and her head push forward toward the Garas. Weejon understood her message immediately.

"We have something to tell you," he said.

The Garas leaned forward and prepared to feign surprise.

Marianne and Weejon joined hands. Then Weejon said, "We are getting married!"

The room filled with cheers, and then Mr. Gara said, "*Sláinte!*"

And then they all drank to the news.

"We want to get married here in your cottage!"

"*Sláinte!*"

And then they all drank to the cottage.

Mrs. Gara had a worried look on her face after that last toast, which they all noticed. Marianne spoke: "What's wrong, Mrs. Gara?"

"The Church will never allow that. They won't bless the wedding unless it is performed in the church with a mass."

"I won't go into any church," Marianne said firmly.

"Don't worry," replied Mr. Gara, "I know a Jesuit."

"*Sláinte!*"

And then they all drank to the Jesuit.

They were all feeling a little tipsy by this time, as none of them was a drinker. Laughter flowed, and the four of them had never felt so close.

"Another toast," Mr. Gara interjected into their conversation, filling each of their glasses. "To poteen!"

"*Sláinte!*"

And then they all drank to poteen.

"Now it's time for us to tell you our surprise." Mrs. Gara nodded to her husband.

"I want to show you our root cellar."

Weejon turned toward Mr. Gara and said, "I didn't know this cottage had a root cellar."

"That's because we don't, exactly," Mrs. Gara answered, grinning.

Marianne and Weejon were now truly confused.

"Follow me." Mr. Gara stood and staggered out the door.

They followed him out and around the cottage toward the back. He stopped near a pile of detritus consisting of old boards and a couple of old wooden crates. Weejon had always thought it was scrap wood for the fireplace. Mr. Gara worked as quickly as his poteen-filled head allowed, to remove the debris and reveal a heavy wooden trapdoor.

Weejon and Marianne followed Mr. Gara past the opened trapdoor and down into the hole. Once their eyes adjusted to the dark, they saw a still in front of them.

"See, it's not a root cellar at all," Mr. Gara exclaimed. "It's a distillery!"

Mrs. Gara added, "And that is the beginning of our surprise."

Marianne and Weejon wondered what this still could possibly have to do with them, and their curiosity was heightened.

"We got the idea a few years ago. We kept it secret from you for this surprise and to protect you in case it was discovered. You could honestly have said you knew nothing about it."

Suddenly Weejon understood some of the unusual smells that sometimes filled the cottage. "Now I know why the chimney smoked even when there was no log burning in the fireplace. I just thought it was more of Mrs. Gara's magic!"

"Oh, it wasn't magic, for there was indeed a fire burning down below us."

Mr. Gara explained that he had learned to make poteen from his da when he was a young man back in Ireland. He went on to say it was considered the best poteen in the whole country. When he came to England, he'd given it up for fear of arrest.

He decided to restart distilling, however, once he came up with a new plan. "Once we came up with the idea we are about to divulge to you, you'll understand. I don't call it moonshine anymore, for there is no moon shining down there. I call it root shine!" Then he chuckled loudly at his own joke.

Weejon was shocked! He'd never thought that Mr. Gara would ever do anything illegal, especially involving alcohol. He'd thought of him as a teetotaler for all those years. "Why would you do this and risk imprisonment?"

"I did it for you," he replied. "Well, now it is for both of you." He bent down toward the ground, reaching for something. He then handed Weejon a heavy leather pouch. "It was worth the risk for this."

Weejon took the satchel and was surprised at its weight. He untied the leather thongs and peered inside. The satchel was full of coins. "There is a small fortune in here!"

"Aye, and it is yours. For both of ye. It's our wedding gift to you."

Marianne and Weejon were overcome. Tears poured down their cheeks. "We can't—," Marianne started to say before she was interrupted.

"Quiet, lass," said Mrs. Gara. "We will say no more about it."

With that said, they all exchanged hugs and decided to toast to poteen one more time.

"Apparently the English around here like poteen as much as the Irish do, and they are willing to pay good money for this particular brand," Mr. Gara added as they left the distillery.

When Marianne arrived back to the manor, she found Sadhbh waiting for her in the kitchen.

"I have a gift for you."

"A gift? For what now?"

"For your wedding, of course."

Marianne sat down at the table. "Jaysus," she said, "it seems everyone knew what we planned before even we did."

"It didn't take a Scotland Yard detective to figure that out," she replied as she slipped toward Marianne a small package wrapped in cloth and tied with a ribbon.

Marianne slowly untied the ribbon and the cloth fell open. She gasped. "Oh my, Sadhbh, these are beautiful!" She held in her hand two polished sterling silver rings. "How ever did you afford to buy these?"

"Oh, they were free. I 'borrowed' them from the manor's silver tray. I don't think the lord and the lady will miss two little dessert spoons." She gave a warm smile like only "sisters" can give to each other. "Then I had the tinker in town form them into these rings with Gaelic knot designs." She gestured with her hands as if to say it had been no trouble at all. "I just promised that I would take care of his laundry at no cost for a while."

They had a good laugh at that, and then Marianne spoke, "I want you to be my maid of honor."

"I would love that!"

Then they stood and hugged. They held each other for a long time.

The wedding was performed the following week. The Jesuit led the ceremony and promised Weejon and Marianne to get a legal marriage license that they could file at their local parish church once they arrived in Ireland.

Mr. Gara served as the best man and wept throughout the ceremony. Afterward he explained that "me bladder must be connected to me eyes."

After the Jesuit left, the five remaining broke out the poteen, sang old Irish songs, and danced away the night.

Near the end of the evening, Mr. Gara spoke: "I have one more gift for you."

He then told the couple that he had a dear friend who had lived in the Wicklow Mountains of Ireland. He had passed away during the famine and left his small cottage to the Garas, as he did not have any surviving relatives. Mr. and Mrs. Gara had spoken about moving back to Ireland, but they eventually decided that their home was in England now, after all these years. They decided they were too old to move, and they'd been told that the cottage in Ireland was going to need a lot of work.

Once again, the Garas brought the newlyweds to tears of joy.

The couple made final plans, bought passage to Dublin, and arranged transport to County Wicklow. This part was exciting, but saying goodbye to the best friends they'd ever known was painful. It was bittersweet, but overall, they all agreed it was more sweet than bitter.

They arrived at the docks in Bristol, ready to board the ship. Weejon, carrying his tool bag, wore his medallion under his shirt. Hidden next to the medallion was the satchel of money. Marianne had nothing but the clothes she was wearing. Hidden beneath those clothes was a growing baby.

Arrival in Ireland

The couple arrived at the Dublin port to begin their new life together. On the ship over, Weejon had decided that he would leave his old name behind; from then on, he would be known as John. There was no one left in Ireland from his family, so he thought it not only practical but symbolic. He did still have the Garas, but he thought they would understand his decision. In any event, Marianne approved of the name change.

The first task was to find a way to Wicklow. Money was not a problem, as John had the satchel of money from the Garas hiding under his shirt. They asked around the port and were eventually directed to a farmer sitting atop a wooden cart. John approached him and asked, "Excuse me, sir. Would you be going to Wicklow?"

"Aye," the farmer replied simply.

"Would you be willing to take us there for a fee?"

"Aye," the man replied while arching his hand, thumb extended, toward the back of his wooden cart.

John and Marianne, relieved, walked toward the back of the cart. John opened the gate and helped his new wife up. As he himself climbed in, he noted that one of the largest pigs he ever laid eyes on took up most of the space in the middle of the cart.

John slammed the gate shut and locked it with pins. The noise woke the pig. Marianne squeezed onto the bench on the left side of the cart, and John was left to squeeze onto the bench on the right side. Sitting across from each other, they just shrugged.

The pig, now wide awake, did not move but stared directly in John's direction as the cart began to roll forward. It continued to stare at him as they rolled along the bumpy road. John tried to look away but couldn't resist looking back to see if the pig was still staring. Indeed, the beast continued to stare right at him.

John knew it was ridiculous, but he started to think about the ham they had eaten at the Garas. He was feeling guilty. Maybe the pig knew. Eventually guilt-stricken enough, John said out loud, "Well, fine, then. I am sorry."

Marianne awoke from her daydreams and asked, "What did you say?"

"Oh, nothing. Just talking to myself." He gave an embarrassed shrug and continued. "I am a little bored and uncomfortable. Let's play a game." (He really just wanted to get his mind off the damn pig.)

"That sounds like a fine idea."

"When I was Weejon, my da would lie on the grass with me, and we would look up at the clouds and try to find different shapes. I loved playing that game with him. Let's do that!"

John slipped off the bench, sat on the floor of the cart, and stretched his legs out across toward Marianne. She copied his position. There was barely enough room for both at the back of the cart. Then they laid their heads back on the side of the cart.

Marianne laughed and then pointed. "There's a scone." She pointed in a different direction. "And over there is a house with a chimney."

John tried hard but at first couldn't find anything. Finally, he did see a shape. It was a pig! Then another! And finally, a third. Giving up on his fate, he admitted, "I see a pig over there."

"Where? I don't see a pig."

But John had already given up and accepted his fate. All the while, the accusatory pig to his right continued to stare.

John was relieved when the farmer finally announced, "We're in Wicklow. Here's where you get out."

John paid the man, and he and Marianne jumped off the back of the cart. When he turned around to close and lock the gate, he could swear that the pig smiled and winked before closing its eyes to return to sleep. John locked the gate and turned away to join Marianne—feeling defeated by a pig, of all things.

They followed the road leading to their new home. Mr. Gara had written down directions for them, complete with landmarks to check off as they walked. Within a few miles, they came upon their new place. It was indeed in need of some fixing up. A lot more than they'd thought.

They walked around the outside and noted many of the stones that needed new mortar and a roof that needed some new thatch. Despite this, they immediately fell in love with the cottage. It was theirs, free and clear. They had enough money from the generous gift from the Garas to do all they needed and then some.

Before entering, John instructed Marianne to wait by the door. He then took a hammer from his toolbox and began walking around the stone cottage again, banging on the stones as he walked. He also was screaming like a banshee. Whenever he walked past a window, he opened the shutters and yelled a little louder. When he completed his circular journey, he stopped in front of Marianne, who stared at him with her arms akimbo.

"What in God's name was that?"

John laughed. "Let's just call it a little ancient Irish country magic." He then opened the door suddenly and said the magic words: "Everybody out!"

From the doors and windows, from under the foundation, and through holes in the roof came a veritable catalogue of Irish tenants, accompanied by a cacophony of squeaks and screeches: a few gray squirrels, a badger, a red fox, several brown rats, and a couple of wood mice.

Marianne smiled in appreciation. "Your magic seemed to work!"

"They were just keeping the place warm for us."

They both had a good laugh. Then suddenly John scooped Marianne up in his arms and carried her across the threshold. She gave a scream of surprise as they entered the dimly lit room. When their eyes adjusted to the darkness, they saw that the only piece of furniture in the cottage was a small wooden table.

John set Marianne gently down on the table and kissed her passionately. They were alone in their new home, and the first thing they did was christen their new abode right there on that small wooden table in the darkness. Afterward, Marianne said simply, "I like this Irish magic better than the previous one."

The next few weeks were a blur of activity, fixing and stocking their new home. They made some inquiries in Wicklow regarding a midwife to deliver their new baby and were directed to a woman named Martha, who had many years of experience and had a solid reputation. They paid her a visit once they were settled.

"Come in," Martha said as she opened the door, "You must be the O'Neils."

"Yes," they replied in unison as they stepped inside. "We are pleased to meet you."

After some further pleasantries, Marianne and Martha entered a separate room. When Martha was finished with her examination, she told Marianne to get dressed and meet her and John in the kitchen. She made them tea as they waited for Marianne's return.

"Both mother and baby are as fit as a fiddle, but there is one concern. The baby is breech."

Martha then explained what a breech baby meant and the risks involved with delivery. She tried to give them some hope that the baby still might right itself, but she knew that the possibility was unlikely. She told them to make sure to get word to her as soon as her pains started.

The next few weeks the couple stayed busy with readying their home for their child. John also went into town and tried to find work. Mr. Gara had told him that with his experience, he was likely to find work in the nearby Avoca mines without difficulty. He even gave him a letter of reference and a mining certificate, proving he had finished his apprenticeship. There was only one stipulation that John insisted on: He would not start work until after their baby was born, as he had to be available to get the midwife when the time came. Since the Avoca managers needed miners, they agreed to the plan with a handshake.

By now the cottage had basic furniture and a roof without leaks. John and Marianne had set up a crib in their bedroom and had a good supply of baby clothes and swaddling cloths. They were ready.

No matter how busy they were, they each took time to write letters back to England. John wrote to Mr. Gara every month to update him and Mrs. Gara on their life. Marianne wrote to Sadhbh similarly.

One morning, while John was on the roof doing some additional repairs on the chimney, he heard his wife call to him. He climbed down the ladder and entered the kitchen. Marianne stood in front of him, slightly bent over, holding her belly.

"*Pog mo thoin!* The pains have started! Time to fetch Martha."

John dropped his tools where he stood and ran through the door toward Wicklow.

THE O'NEIL

A NOVEL

The O'Neil's Childhood

The O'Neil's early years were idyllic. The memories of his parents were not his. He had been born without problematic concerns from his parents' past experiences, born in a sturdy Irish cottage with a watertight thatched roof, surrounded by a stone wall and green grass, plenty of food on the table, and two parents who loved him. Those were all the things anyone needed for an idyll.

His ma breastfed him well, and soon he had more fat on him than most Irish lads his age. His ma credited that to herself being well fed from the income they had from John's work at the Avoca mines six days a week and from their garden, which was her responsibility. Not only did they have plenty of food, but they also had the peace of mind because of the money left over from the Garas' generous gift.

Marianne lived for The O'Neil. This, apparently, did not go unnoticed by the little lad, for he seemed to repay the debt daily. His currency was giving his parents the joy that only a child can give a parent. A joy that reminds parents of the wonders of the world around them. A joy that is forgotten by many adults. A joy that seems to have an expiration date and dissolves as one ages. The O'Neil gave this joy back to his parents each day, and they soaked it in. They both knew that this was the magic of childhood recaptured.

His ma was very busy as she took responsibility for keeping their cottage in tip-top shape, putting food on the table for her men and tending their garden. John worked long hours at the mines but always had time for his son in the evenings and on Sundays. The O'Neil was always their priority.

THE O'NEIL

Once The O'Neil was old enough to walk, his ma included him in everything she did throughout the day. She would sit him next to her as she cooked or have him carry little things for her. He seemed so proud of himself. She didn't have the heart to tell him that he made her work less efficient by half.

His true love, though, was being in the garden with her. He loved to be outside, and that made him happiest. Once he was old enough to walk well, he never seemed to stop unless he was sleeping. His ma spent a good portion of the day chasing after him. His favorite destination was the old drystone wall surrounding their cottage. It seemed to be magnetic to him. He made a beeline to it the minute the cottage door opened. His ma was grateful that it penned him in, or God only knows how far he would get before she could catch him. He had started walking by nine months, and by a year he could run quite well.

Once he got to the wall, he would bend down as if he were inspecting it and slowly walk along it until something caught his attention. Then he would plop down and spend quite a while sitting next to it, pulling off small stones and looking for little creatures. He could do this for hours. Once Marianne realized this was his pattern, she was less worried about chasing him. She would walk out to him every so often to talk with him and let him show her the various treasures he had found.

"*Mo gra*," she greeted him as she sat in the turf next to him, "what do you have there?"

He would smile in response, babble a few things, and then hand her his finds. They usually consisted of a collection of insects, shiny stones, and a worm or two.

"Look how this little guy wiggles!" his ma would say as she held the gifted worm.

The O'Neil's face lit up, and he smiled broadly with pride.

Some of his finds fared better than others. The rocks never seemed to mind his toddler grip, but the living things did not fare as well at times. His ma loved sitting there in the grass next to him, and sometimes she forgot all about chores and just enjoyed this time with her son.

Once he started to speak, he would greet his da at the door when he returned home from work and exclaim, "I cleaned!"

John would look toward his wife and wink, then reply, "Well, it looks wonderful!" as he scooped his son up for a big hug.

The O'Neil's desire for wandering only increased as his walking skills improved. He could see things that seemed invisible to adults. He graduated to being able to catch grasshoppers and mice. It seemed that the old drystone wall held more creatures than his ma could have imagined.

As The O'Neil got older, his ma let him expand his explorations beyond the stone wall out into the nearby tree line. The expansion gave his hunting skills a bigger challenge. Now he could find even more creatures to bring home to show his ma. He would return with salamanders, mice, voles, and even a rabbit. She did not understand how he did it.

One day he came back with a young rabbit wrapped in his arms to show his mother. "Little one," she asked, "how did you catch this rabbit. They are fast and hard to capture."

"I just asked his ma if I could take him to show you, and I promised to bring him back."

"You talk to the animals?"

"Oh yes. I wouldn't just take him without asking."

His ma asked nothing further, but she was intrigued, to say the least. She held the rabbit, who seemed to suddenly want to flee. She gave him a few strokes and then handed him back to her son. The rabbit seemed to calm in the boy's arms.

"I have to bring him back now," The O'Neil said as he walked back toward the woods.

It was the fox that introduced The O'Neil to his ma's favorite curse word. One nice soft day, he came bounding up toward the cottage with a young fox held securely in his arms. As his ma turned toward him, she exclaimed, "*Pog mo thoin!*" Immediately realizing what she said, she clamped her hand over her mouth as if she could stop the words from reaching her son. She hoped he did not hear her. "What is that?!" she asked.

The O'Neil looked down at the fox in his arms and then back toward his ma. "It's a fox, ma."

"Well, I can see that, but how did you get a fox?"

"They live over there in the woods."

"They?"

"Yes, her ma and a brother."

"How did you catch a fox?"

"I've been visiting them every day for a long time now and have been asking to take her to show you, and her ma finally consented."

"You talk to the foxes too?"

The O'Neil didn't reply but just wrinkled his eyebrows as if confused by the question. "You can't hold her," he said, "but you can pet her. She is soft."

His ma, still confused by his find, approached cautiously and petted the fox a few times.

"I have to bring her back now."

"Yes, I think that's a good idea," his mother replied, relieved by the idea. "I think I will go with you. I would like to meet her ma."

"Oh, she won't want you to do that. She is very shy."

"I will stay back a bit. I would at least like to know where our neighbors are living."

The O'Neil simply replied, "That would be fine."

The O'Neil led her back to the woods. She stayed back a way as he approached a large rock and gently set down the little fox, who scurried toward the rock and disappeared into her den.

Marianne whispered to herself, "*Pog mo thoin*, if he comes home with a snake someday, then for sure I will know he has some kind of magical power."

That night The O'Neil was even more excited to greet his da at the door and to tell him about his day. When John stepped over the threshold, his son ran to him and said, "*Pog mo thoin!*"

John's mouth fell open, and he gave his wife a side glance. Her face blushed a fiery red. Once the initial shock wore off, he tried to hold back laughing along with his wife. The O'Neil then told his da about his new fox friends. John was incredulous at first, but Marianne supported the boy's story. John felt the same as Marianne that their son did have some kind of magic within him.

As time went on, The O'Neil was referred to by many different terms of endearment, such as mo gra, laddie, little one, and honey, but the most common nickname and the one that stuck was Theo. It was just easier to say than The O'Neil. Although this became the name used by his parents, later in life and anyone else besides his parents only ever used his full name, The O'Neil. As he got older and learned the story of his name, The O'Neil, he would become very proud of it and would take offense to anything else.

Theo loved spending time with his da. On the long summer days in Ireland, there was plenty of daylight left in the evenings. Their favorite thing to do together was exploring the woods nearby. Theo loved showing his da where his various animal friends resided. They would lift rocks and search out other small creatures.

John taught Theo all he knew about the various living things around them. He taught his son about the trees, including which ones were magical, and about which plants could be eaten by either animals or people.

"Theo, we need to return to the cottage."

Theo replied in a whining voice, "Please, da, can't we stay a little longer?"

"No, it's going to rain hard very soon."

"How do you know that, da?" Theo replied with a puzzlement showing on his face.

"Look, the leaves are getting very nervous." John was pointing to the rapidly rustling leaves on the trees surrounding them.

"I see, da." So, Theo followed his da down the worn path back to the cottage.

Another favorite activity was to lie on the grass on those rare days without rain or mist and to look at the clouds. They would identify shapes and point them out to each other. John was relieved that he never once saw another pig up there. The curse seemed to have been broken!

Theo once asked his da about the medallion he wore. John explained that it had been given to him by Theo's granda and that someday he would give it to Theo. "It's written in Gaelic. It means to always be strong and to grow toward the light." John explained its meaning and said it in Gaelic for Theo to hear in his native language. It was at that moment that he realized it was time for Theo to start learning Gaelic along with arithmetic, reading, and the history of the Irish people.

He spoke with Marianne later that night, and they developed an educational plan for their son. Marianne would teach him reading and arithmetic while John took care of history and Gaelic. They decided they would start to speak more Gaelic around the house, but they had to be careful never to use Gaelic when they went to Wicklow, for the language was still outlawed by their English overlords.

The three of them did especially enjoy going into Wicklow. It was, of course, the biggest city that Theo had ever seen. He couldn't believe the number of people, horses, mules, and buildings so much different from their cottage. They tried to get there about once a month to pick up supplies and to let Theo wonder at the sights around him. They always got Theo a funnel cake, which was the best food he'd ever tasted.

Theo especially liked going to the Black Castle ruins. It was the most ancient castle in the area, built by the Norman English around the twelfth century. It had frequently been attacked by local chieftains of the O'Byrne and O'Toole clans. They succeeded in finally destroying it in 1301. John used the ruins as an example of the will of the Irish people to regain their land back from the English. The clans had eventually won against overwhelming odds. As his da told him the story as if he were there, full of details and Irish humor, Theo was rapt with attention. He was impressed very much by these stories.

THE O'NEIL

Theo's Education

It became clear as Theo grew older that not only was his body growing strong, so was his mind. By the time he was six, he simply outpaced his parents' ability to teach him. They knew that he had an insatiable desire for more knowledge, and they wanted to feed it. That gave them an idea.

In their next letter to the Garas, they would ask if they approved of using the rest of their gifted money for The O'Neil's education. The response back, of course, was an overwhelming AYE!

John began making enquiries at work and whenever they were in Wicklow. There was a free school that had been started by Erasmus Smith. The problems with that school were that Smith was a Protestant, the school required teaching only English, and they prayed and sang only in the Protestant traditions. This was more than John could bear. He was not a devout Catholic by any means, but he still blamed the English for both the death of his family as well as the incarceration of his country.

There was a Catholic education system that was free to those who couldn't pay—or the cost was matched to the family's ability to pay. These schools also would not have been the best choice; John didn't want Theo indoctrinated too deeply in the Catholic traditions either. The schools generally conformed to the rules placed on them by the Protestant English ("United Kingdom") government and refused to teach Gaelic, but they did still teach Catholic doctrine. Though, with the advent of the national school system, Catholic schools were allowed to operate but could not display religious icons or pictures and had to separate general education from their religion. The schools accepted these restrictions, as they figured the children could get indoctrinated enough on Sundays.

There were also private schools, but the cost of those would all too quickly burn up the savings John and Marianne had. They had a decision to make for Theo. They decided that the enrollment in the Catholic school system would be the compromise.

"So, that's the decision?" Marianne asked.

"I think that's best, so we will arrange it next week when we go to Wicklow. I have another idea, though, too. I think we need to find a Jesuit to add some more flavoring to his education."

"That's a good idea. It was a traveling Jesuit who taught me some Gaelic." She subconsciously placed her hand over her heart before continuing. "They are all rebels in their own way," she said, laughing.

They got Theo enrolled in the school the following weekend, and they were lucky with the issue of finding a Jesuit. The new field of chemistry was beginning to make its way into the curriculum of many schools. It was going to be taught only at the high school level, but the new chemistry teacher was an Irish Jesuit priest, Father Doran. On the next trip to Wicklow, they set up a meeting with Father Doran.

"Good morning, Father," said John, extending his hand and slightly bowing his head.

Father Doran extended his hand and gripped John's, replying, "It's nice to meet you." He then turned toward Marianne and bowed his head in greeting to her as well before turning toward Theo.

"So, you must be the lad looking for an education."

"Yes, Father, my name is The O'Neil."

"The O'Neil? Well, that is a unique name." He scratched his head. "How did you come to be called that?"

"It's not a nickname. It's my given name."

Father Doran, eyebrows raised, looked to John and then Marianne, and they nodded back to him.

"Well, The O'Neil, I am going to speak with your parents about your education and get back to you." He pointed Theo toward a chair along the wall, and the boy walked over, sat down, and looked around the spacious, well-furnished office.

"I know you have your son enrolled in our school already," the priest addressed the parents in a low voice. "So why do you need me?"

"We need you for the Gaelic." John's voice was even more hushed.

"I see." Father Doran rubbed his chin.

"We taught him all we could about Irish history and whatever Gaelic we knew, but we don't know enough to give him a truly *green tongu*e," John replied, winking at the priest.

"Well, I think I can be discreet enough to teach him some of that outlawed language, but there will be a cost."

Marianne looked at John, brow furrowed in worry as she wondered if they could afford it. John stared at the Jesuit priest, waiting for his next sentence.

"I will require a bottle of Irish whiskey every month throughout the school year. Preferably a different one each month, so my palate does not become bored." He laughed heartily.

Marianne and John broke out in chuckles. "That I can certainly afford!" John said. "Thanks, Father." He and Father Doran shook on that deal.

So, Theo's education was arranged: He would begin the following Monday. He would walk with his da toward the mines and get dropped off at the school. When the school day was over, Theo would walk to the mines and join his da as his unofficial (and unpaid) apprentice three days a week. The other three days were his Gaelic lessons, disguised as "tutoring." On those days his da would walk to the school to pick him up, and they would walk home together. Schools in County Wicklow required attendance six days a week, but the students did get out earlier on Saturdays. John worked six full days a week, including Saturday. So, on that day, Theo walked to the mines after school and spent the whole afternoon working alongside his da.

Not only did Theo get an academic education during these years, but he learned mining from one of the best miners in Ireland. He especially liked Saturdays because he spent much more time in the mines with his da. During these years the two became very close. They passed the times on the long walks to and from his school talking. Much of the time they reviewed his lessons and spoke as best they could together in Gaelic in order to practice their native tongue. Some of the time was just talking about nothing and everything all at once. Theo would look back on these days later as the best times of his life.

Marianne would greet her men at the door and always had a big kiss for her husband and a big hug for Theo. She would have a hot meal ready for them. They spent the rest of the evening either in the yard if the weather was fair or inside near the fire if it was not so fair. They would talk and read, and the parents would help Theo with his homework. Life during these years was perfect.

Theo was an imposing presence in his school. Although he was a few years younger than some of his classmates, he was bigger both in size and presence. With a name like The O'Neil, one would think he would have been bullied. That never happened, however. There was something about Theo that kept anyone from trying.

Maybe it was his presence or maybe it was just his upbringing, but Theo did not tolerate the bullying of anyone else either. He stepped right in if anyone was being bullied, and he put an end to it. Most bullies just backed down, but there were a few who tried to test him. It was not without sacrifice that Theo stepped in, for he did end up with a bloody nose or two as well as some scrapes and bruises. He always prevailed because he had the persistence of the good. His da always told him that evil is strong but has a weakness. Its weakness is impatience. Goodness's strength is that it is patient. It never gives up and always wins in the end. Theo followed this advice. He was tenacious when he knew he was doing the right thing.

Theo developed quite a reputation around the school. He was one of the best students—in fact, perhaps he was gifted. He was secretly referred to as the Enforcer by the teachers in the school for his work at keeping the bullies at bay.

Theo's reputation did not escape Father Doran's notice either. That reputation gave the priest an idea. He was waiting for John one morning when he was dropping Theo off. "John, I wanted to talk to you about The O'Neil."

"Aye, Father, what did he do?"

Father Doran laughed and then said, "Nothing bad, that's for sure. Quite the opposite. He's one of our 'strongest' students."

John did not get the double meaning of Father Doran's words, but his chest filled with pride. "Is he now?"

"Aye, he is indeed." The priest gestured toward a book on chemistry on his desk. "I have a proposal for you to think about. As you know, I am assigned to teach the newly developed course of chemistry, and I would like to start teaching The O'Neil."

"I don't know anything about che-chemistry, but if you think it's important for him to learn it, then I think my wife and I would be happy to have him learn it."

"Chemistry is going to be the future of the modern world. I see endless possibilities for students of chemistry. Your son will gain a great benefit from this knowledge." He paused to emphasize what he was about to say. "But there is a cost."

"We don't have much money left for his education, Father, but if we can afford it, we surely will be happy to pay."

Father Doran laughed out loud. "No, the cost is not in money. It's just that the chemistry lessons will cut into his Gaelic instruction. I will be teaching two courses in the same amount of time."

"I see." John, unsure, closed his mouth tightly and sucked in his left cheek. "Well, I will talk to Marianne and let you know tomorrow." He turned to leave, replacing his cap onto his head, but then he paused and turned back around toward Father Doran. "I take you at your word, and if this chemistry thing is important, then I am all for it, and I think Marianne will agree."

John said goodbye to Father Doran and then said to his son, "Enjoy the school day. I will see you later at the mines." He took a few steps away before remembering he had something for Father Doran. "Father, I forgot to give you this." He reached into his lunch pail, pulled out a bottle of Powers Whiskey, and handed it over to the priest.

"Powers! I was hoping I would get one of these soon. One of my favorites." He lifted the bottle to his lips, placed a warm kiss on it, smiled, and said, "Thanks!"

John nodded and smiled as he turned and silently walked away.

Theo began his chemistry instruction the next time he met with Father Doran. He was a natural and soaked it up. He found the subject fascinating. He never told his da this, but on some days, he asked to just learn chemistry and to skip Gaelic altogether.

His da was also curious about this new field of study. He could tell that Theo was very excited about it, and their walks were now filled with a lot of chemistry talk. John had some trouble following all of it, but he agreed that it seemed fascinating. He began to pick up some of the subject. It seemed that Theo was a natural teacher as well as a student.

The O'Neil became Father Doran's best student in no time, and this reputation also began to grow around the school. The reputation grew not only around the school but around the whole area of Wicklow.

A reputation for chemistry expertise would generally have been a good thing, but there were some in the Wicklow area who did not have the best of intentions. A new movement was starting around Ireland, and it seemed to be centered in County Wicklow. There was a growing group of rebels who were fed up with their subjugation by the English and became impatient with finding a political solution. They wanted their freedom, and they wanted it now.

A NOVEL

The Rebels

The Gannon brothers were a problem looking for a solution. They lived together in County Wicklow. They had been self-educated on the streets of Dublin. The oldest, Mickey, seemed to be their leader, and his two brothers, Kelly and Bairre, looked to him for guidance. Mickey was as different from his younger siblings as siblings could be. He was quite tall, had dark hair, had freckled skin, and always seemed to have a bit of a sunburn. Kelly and Bairre both had blond hair that hung much closer to the ground than their sibling's. They also had tanned, freckleless skin. People prone to gossip in County Wicklow always suspected that they had a different father than Mickey's, and knowing their mother's history, they may have been right.

The Gannons had been born to parents who also knew all about the streets. Their da was tall and heavily muscled. He was mean, with an intimidating presence. These traits landed him a job as the enforcer at a Dublin brothel. It was there that he met his wife, one of the prostitutes at said brothel. She was as tough as he, and maybe that's what attracted him to her. She soon became pregnant, and once she could no longer hide that fact, she was sent away from the brothel. Mr. Gannon did not appreciate this and decided he would let them know exactly how he felt. He wouldn't hit a woman, so he pummeled the madam's bodyguard instead. He thought this was a good way to let them know that he quit.

The Gannon family had fled to Wicklow to start a new life. They started out as happy as any other family in Wicklow, but it was not long before life began to turn dark. The father began to drink, and his drinking eventually became more important than his work and family. This created a big strain between the Gannon brothers' parents. Mr. Gannon started to find work on the streets, work that was not always legal. Once the streets get into your veins, it becomes more of an addiction than the alcohol itself. He began to associate with the worst characters in the town and was seen less and less by his family, eventually vanishing without a trace.

Mrs. Gannon, herself with a dark soul within her, made do with her own work on the streets of Wicklow. Her work, however, did not at first turn out so well, as she ran into some of the darkest souls of Wicklow. Nonetheless, she made some decent wages, and she cared for her family with the money she earned on her back and knees. The children, now old enough to understand what was happening to their mother, shook in fear when she came home with a bruised and bloody face. Gradually the darkness took her, and she too began to drink. Drinking to relieve her pain and to forget the future that was no more. Once she was sick of the violence she was suffering, she moved back to Dublin to join a brothel under the protection of a madam. She either forgot to tell her children—or, more likely, she couldn't face telling them that she could not take them with her.

The Gannon boys, now in their early teen years, waited for her for two days before accepting the fact that she too had abandoned them. They each swore a blood oath that they would not ever be separated and that they would not ever live in an orphanage. They took what they needed from their home and headed into the mountains with a confidence that they had learned from surviving on the streets of Wicklow.

They had been on their own anyway over the past four or five years, while their mother had slowly been slipping away from them. They were survivors, and they felt comfortable surviving on the streets. Maybe Mickey had learned a few things from their da, or maybe his survival knowledge was just inherited. He passed on this knowledge to his younger siblings as they aged. They all survived by pickpocketing, robbing, scamming, and begging. They had lived in the shadows and away from notice while residing right in the center of the town. In the mountains, however, they could live even more in the shadows and away from being found out. Their jobs would not change, only their home base.

"This is the cave that I told yous about," Mickey said as he pulled some branches away from the opening.

His brothers peered over his shoulder and shuddered. "Are you sure it's safe?" asked Kelly.

"Yeah, I've been in here many times. I would come up here to get away from Ma and Da fighting." He spread his left arm toward the now-cleared entrance to guide them in. "I would have taken you two, but yous were too little to travel then."

The trio entered the cave and looked around. Mickey told the pair behind him, "Grab some wood, and we'll get a fire going. Then we can light these oil lamps and set up our new home."

They unloaded what they carried into the mouth of the cave and then set off into the woods. When they returned with firewood, Mickey piled the pieces and then got to work with his flint to light a fire.

The cave was a step up from living with their parents. They were free, and they had enough to eat, as they were quite good at procuring food through whatever means were necessary. They lacked only one thing: They lacked purpose. But as fate does sometimes come knocking, it came knocking shortly after they moved into their new home.

While in town "foraging" one day, Mickey saw a number of placards that were posted throughout the town. He ripped one down and ran home to show it to his brothers. He had to read it to them, as he was the only one of the brothers who was literate. "Look at this!"

Kelly and Bairre crowded around him, looking at the cipher written on the placard.

Mickey read aloud: "'We are looking for patriots to the cause of Irish freedom. We no longer accept the brutal English rule and are going to start fighting for freedom. Political means have failed. Now it's time to fight, like the Society of United Irishmen did and like Wolfe Tone did. If you want to join us, draw an *X* on the wall below this placard.'"

Kelly and Bairre both nodded their heads, wondering whether this might be an exciting job. They asked, "Will we get paid?"

"I am not sure, but when we meet, we will find out all the details. We can be rebels! This will be fun."

"Well, let's go draw an *X*!" they shouted in reply.

"I already took care of it." He took a bow toward his brothers.

They carried on with their normal routine and waited, unsure of how or when they would be contacted.

Several weeks later the Gannon brothers received their answer from the rebels. They had just returned from foraging pockets in Wicklow when they were startled by a visitor hidden in their cave. When they came in from the brightness of the day, the cave was darker than usual despite the still-burning oil lamps. Before their eyes could adjust to the change, they heard a voice out of the darkness: "Welcome home, boys!"

The three Gannon brothers nearly jumped out of their skin. They all yelped and thought for sure there was a peeler waiting to nick them. As the dimness dissolved into light, however, a shadowy figure appeared before them. He wore all black and a cap atop a face that was masked by a piece of cloth. He surely was no constable.

Mickey breathed a sigh of relief. "You scared the bejabbers out of us!"

The moment of relief was suddenly replaced by dread as Mickey wondered if this shadowy figure would turn out to be more dangerous than a peeler. His brothers came to the same conclusion, and they all reflexively backed up a few steps toward the cave entrance.

The stranger, seeing their reaction, reassured them. "Don't worry. I am here just to deliver a message."

The brothers stopped their backsteps, stood right where they were, and waited for more. And if it was true that this visitor was a "messenger," then they were about to hear where their new future was heading. Mickey surmised that this mysterious stranger might be the fork in the road of their lives. The brothers slowly sat down, following the lead of the stranger.

"We spent the past few weeks investigating you," the visitor said. "You have quite the reputation among the dark elements of Wicklow. We know all about your petty criminal enterprise."

With those words, the brothers felt their stomachs in their throats. Did this mean they would surely be rejected? Their shoulders sagged.

The shadowy figure laughed long and hard at their expressions. Then: "The expressions on your faces are precious. Did you think that your résumé disqualified you? Don't you understand that you're the exact type we need?" He shook his head at their stupidity, giving him second thoughts about recruiting them. "We also need your cave."

After a pause for the stranger's message to sink in, the Gannons jumped up, yelped, and gave back-slapping hugs to one another. They were at first overjoyed, but once the initial excitement wore off, Mickey wondered what the stranger had meant by the last part about their cave and what that would mean for their living arrangements.

"Very well now," said the stranger, "calm down and listen to the terms before you jump for joy. This is a give-and-take relationship, and it has some costs for both of us." He sat on one of the Gannons' rickety chairs and continued: "We need this cave to store weapons and maybe hide one of our men from time to time."

Mickey asked, "Then, where will we live?"

"We have an offer for you." He gestured for them to move in closer. "Our group will give you a small flat right in downtown Wicklow." He winced in disgust at the smiles growing on their faces. "It's from there that you can continue your petty criminal activity." The disgust in his voice was obvious.

The Gannon brothers missed the disgust, however, and they smiled broadly at the thought of being back in town. Town would be much more convenient for continuing their careers in supporting themselves.

"But remember," the stranger warned, "our group is your priority. When we need you, you will drop whatever it is you're doing and come running." He stood and took a few steps toward the cave's opening. As he reached the exit, he turned back and pointed to a dark corner. "I left three guns back there for you." He briefly looked each one of them in the eye. "Have you ever held a gun before?"

The brothers, embarrassed, looked blankly at one another. Then Mickey spoke, "Well, er, umm, no."

"I didn't think so. We begin training Sunday morning. I will return then." He punctuated his remark by pointing at the group. "We'll find a place on the other side of the mountain to keep the sounds from reaching town. Sunday morning is also best because all the Catholics around here will be off the streets and tucked nicely away in church, singing like injured parakeets to loud organ music." Then he stepped through the exit and vanished.

The brothers went right for the guns. Three pistols, neatly wrapped in oilcloth, sat in the back of their cave. They each took one and immediately pretended to be shooting at one another and at imaginary constables. They neglected to check if the pistols were loaded as they played with them, even pulling the triggers. The guns made them feel powerful. The mysterious stranger had made sure that the guns had no bullets before leaving them in the care of these *eejits*. He'd had foresight, knowing that a round going off in the confines of the cave would have created a disaster with ricochets.

What the brothers didn't know was that they were playing with the latest revolvers produced by Samuel Colt. The rebels' main supply of weapons at this time came from America.

Sunday morning arrived. The Gannon brothers awoke to the smell of cigarette smoke. Once they realized the presence of another person in their cave, they jumped up, guns in their hands, pointing to the visitor, the mystery man, face covered with a bandana with only dark eyes peering at them. He was sitting patiently on the floor of the cave, smoking. He laughed vigorously at the scene, knowing full well that the pistols were not loaded.

"Calm down," he said once he stopped laughing. "I am here to start your training." He stubbed out his cigarette on the cave floor, stood, and beckoned them to follow.

He led them on a small path across the top of the mountain to a small clearing on the back side, away from town. In the clearing were various targets, previously arranged.

The stranger, now instructor, first showed the brothers the various parts of the guns and how to load them, emphasizing their safe handling. "Treat these pistols as if they are always loaded, even if you think you know they are empty. If you ever point it at someone, it means you plan to kill him."

The brothers had really never considered killing another human. They had been responsible for many different crimes through the years, but taking another life had never been one of them. At least, not yet. As the reality of the situation set in, there was a collective gulp.

They spent a few hours on their training, including some actual target shooting. It was thrilling for them to fire the weapons for the first time. At the end of the morning session, they were taught how to clean and store the weapons safely.

The stranger determined that Mickey was the best shot of the three. He seemed to have some natural talent. Mickey's two brothers would take more work. The stranger would keep that in mind when it was time for their first assignment.

When they were finished for the day, they walked back to the cave. The stranger instructed the brothers to return the guns to their hiding spot. He told them strictly that they were never to take the guns with them into town. There would be dire consequences if they did that. They must consider this a rule chiseled in stone. He explained that if the authorities were ever to find the guns, the entire effort for Irish freedom might be undone.

After the guns were stored, the stranger told the brothers to grab whatever they wanted to take to their new place. They wouldn't need furniture, as the flat was already furnished. They grabbed their few meager belongings and followed the stranger down the trail toward Wicklow. At the edge of the woods, the stranger stopped. "I leave here." He pointed to his face covering. "I can't go into town looking like this."

Mickey reached out his hand toward the man. "I just wanted to thank you for training us."

The hand was ignored.

Mickey sheepishly pulled his hand back and asked, "What is your name? What do we call you?"

"You don't call me anything, because I don't exist. The less we know about the others in our group, the best for all of us. So never ask me that again," he replied resolutely. Then he disappeared into the trees.

The brothers, not sure what to do next, walked into town. Eventually, a woman who reminded them of their mother approached and, waving a cigarette held between her fingers in front of them, asked, "Do you have a light?"

Kelly, always the ladies' man of the bunch, had the cigarette lit before his brothers knew what was happening.

"Follow me," she stated in a sultry voice. She sashayed down the street, and the brothers followed her into a dark alleyway. She stopped by a door and turned toward them. "This is your new home."

She opened the door and then walked back off toward the street.

The brothers excitedly filed in through the door, into their new place. The dank flat would have disgusted anyone else, but not them. After their time living in a cave, this place seemed like a mansion.

They entered a small kitchen with a potbelly stove. Against another wall in the kitchen was a sink with a water pump. Off to the other side was a sitting room with well-worn wooden chairs set up along some boards over sawhorses.

They stepped through a doorway into a bedroom with three straw mattresses laid out on the floor. If they weren't excitedly chattering, they might have noticed the lice and bedbugs crawling through the straw. In the corner was a metal horse trough, which was to serve as their bathtub.

There was a door leading from this room to a small garden. This was a "garden" only in the sense that it was outside the house because the only thing growing back there was an outhouse. It was to be shared with the several residents in the complex of apartments.

"We have our own place in town!" Bairre exclaimed as the brothers gave one another hugs.

Kelly jumped onto one of the mattresses closest to the door (and the outhouse). "This one is to be mine!" he said through the dust cloud his jump had created.

They unpacked their meager belongings and settled into their new flat, which was in a much more convenient location for their life of petty crime. The only commitment they had so far was training on Sundays. They decided among themselves that they would call that training a "mass." It made them giddy using a code word, as though they were part of a secret brotherhood. What they didn't yet realize is just what type of secret brotherhood they had joined. They made sure to be prompt in attending their "mass," partly due to fear of losing their living space and partly because they feared the stranger they had met.

Their Sunday training was a repetition of target practice, concealing a weapon, cleaning said weapon, and even some Irish history to motivate them to the cause. The history stressed the crimes of the English against the Irish people. They learned about the Society of United Irishmen and the rebellion of 1798, inspired by Wolfe Tone. They studied the tactics that had led to failure of the previous rebellions so that those mistakes would not be repeated. They were taught about Michael Dwyer and the guerilla campaign of 1799 to 1803, led right there from the Wicklow Mountains. They learned the names Robert Emmett and Anne Devlin, Michael Dwyer's cousin, and about the roles they played in the fight for Irish freedom. They were surprised to hear that the group they joined were remnants of that same Society of United Irishmen. They were now reviving the fight for freedom.

"Are we going to use these guns in a coordinated attack against the English?" Mickey asked while spinning the Colt's barrel.

"Are you daft, man? These are just a means to a bigger end." He stared in disgust at their limited understanding of their role in the Brotherhood. "But we all need to be trained in their use. Just in case."

"What's the end?"

"The beginning of the end is a guerilla campaign of terror. That will even the odds a bit and over time bring the English to their knees." He lowered his voice to just above a whisper before revealing anything more. "That brings me to your first assignment." He gestured for them to take a seat on the logs scattered around the clearing. "We plan to target both the police and the rich Protestant landowners who stole land from the Irish people." He paused. "We are not going to use guns. We are going to use explosives!"

The brothers remained silent, barely breathing, and looked at one another. They were beginning to realize that they may have jumped in over their heads.

The masked stranger saw their reaction and stated firmly, "You're not afraid, I hope. Remember our deal and the nice flat we supplied?" He stood, puffing out his chest in a threatening manner. "This is not Sunday school. This is serious business, and the fate of the Irish people hangs in the balance. Our organization does not allow deserters." He repeatedly slammed his fist into an open palm as if warming up for a fight. "Believe me when I say you will not have a very long life if you decide to quit."

The brothers paled, their mouths drying so much that they could not speak. They all just nodded.

"That's better. I am glad you're fully on board." He relaxed his body and stopped pounding his fist. "So, your first assignment will be to find out what you can about the Avoca mines. Find out what kind of protection measures they have to guard against theft and where they store their explosives."

The brothers nodded.

"Something else we need is someone familiar with explosives. So far, we have had no luck convincing a miner to join our cause."

Bairre spoke up: "There's rumor of an adolescent attending the Catholic school in Wicklow who is supposed to be some kind of genius. He might know a thing or two about explosives, and his da is a miner at the Avoca mines, so that could be a two for the price of one."

"Well done! That's what we need from you." He reached out and patted Bairre on the shoulder. "To deserve what we've given you, keep your ears open. Report back next week about what you can find out about the mines and this adolescent 'genius.'" Abruptly, he then disappeared down the path into the woods.

The brothers stored their weapons back in the cave and filed down the path back to Wicklow.

THE O'NEIL

THEO AND THE REBELS

The Gannon brothers came up with a plan to recruit this lad they had been hearing so much about. Bairre, being the youngest and closest to the age of the lad, was selected to meet him and hopefully recruit him. The other two would take care of the surveillance of the mines.

Their years of swindling people and other petty criminal activity had prepared them well for this new endeavor. Each of them liked nothing more than living in the shadows and pretending to be someone he was not.

Bairre waited outside the school for the lad. He spent a few days just observing, making sure he was not spotted. He figured out the lad's schedule and route. It appeared that on some days, a large older man, probably his da, met him. On those days, the lad got out of school later. On the days he got out earlier, he was alone. It seemed that there was a repeating routine, which would make Bairre's plan easier. He wanted to meet the lad alone and avoid encountering the big guy. He noticed that there was some resemblance of this man to his brother Mickey, although Mickey was not as muscular.

Once Bairre had the lad's schedule, he next needed a plan to meet him. He wandered around Wicklow as deep in thought as he was capable of. He occasionally would grin to himself as he thought this might be his best trickery ever.

Near dusk one night, as he passed by a small farm on the outskirts of Wicklow, the idea hit him. Parked at the edge of the farm was a small cart. It was filled with miscellaneous junk and tools and was covered with an oilcloth. He glanced around and, seeing no one, he grabbed the rope attached to the front of the cart and pulled it quickly down the road. He found a nice patch of woods nearby and decided he would stash the cart there until it was needed. He covered it with branches and leaves to keep it hidden. Tomorrow would be the day to make his move.

He showed up early to retrieve the cart because he needed to do some preparation. He pulled the cart toward the school, stopping around the corner from it, just out of sight. He had added a large rock to the cart when he retrieved it, which he now put to use. He climbed under the cart and used the rock to strike the back wooden axle. The wood broke easily, as it was rotted. He placed the two wheels into the cart. He picked up the back of the cart and pushed it along the street, stopping near the school. He then waited. He kept a close watch on the school. Once Bairre saw the lad coming his way, he lifted the cart and pushed it along. He made a good show of struggling to lift and push the cart along.

"Fair day, sir," Theo said as he walked by Bairre.

"It would be if I weren't in a pickle," replied Bairre. "My axle broke, and I still have a few miles to go to deliver this scrap metal."

Theo paused, feeling sorry for this stranger's situation. "Can I help?"

Bairre set the cart down and wiped the sweat from his forehead onto his sleeve. "Short of helping me pull this cart while I lift the back up for the next few miles, I don't know what you could do."

"I have an idea." Theo stepped toward the cart. He rummaged through the cart, picking up various pieces of metal. He looked at each as he turned it over in his hands. He stopped when he found two pickaxes. "This should work," he said out loud to no one. He threaded one end of each of the pickaxes through the opening that previously held the axle. He found some rope and tied the handles securely together above the cart. The result looked a bit ridiculous, as if the cart had horns. Theo then slipped the wheels onto the other side of the pickaxes. The curve of the pickaxes helped to keep the wheel in place, but he twisted some metal wire around the end to make sure the wheels stayed put.

Theo then turned toward Bairre while wiping his dirty hands off on his pants. "There you go. That should get you to your destination at least."

Bairre looked over the work. "You're a genius! I never would have thought of that."

"I am glad to have helped."

"My name is Wolfe," Bairre lied as he reached out his hand to Theo.

"I am The O'Neil." He shook hands with his new acquaintance. "You have an interesting first name. Were you named after Wolfe Tone?"

"Yes, I was, and I do consider him one of my heroes. I think the Irish could use another Wolfe Tone." "Wolfe" gathered up the ropes in front of the cart as he continued: "You have an interesting nickname, yourself. How did you come to be known as that?"

"It's not a nickname, it's my given name."

Bairre was surprised but just nodded.

Theo continued: "Aye, I think we do need another Wolfe Tone. My da taught me a lot about him and about other heroes of the fight for Irish freedom."

"I recently met some men in the Irish Republican Brotherhood, and they asked me to join, so I did. Now I know I am continuing the fight for freedom." He raised his chin to show his pride. "They might be willing to let you join too if you're interested. Even at your age, there might be something you could offer them."

"I am not sure about that. I doubt my da would approve."

"Well, you can think about it." Bairre turned and planted his feet in anticipation of rolling the cart forward. "I come by this way often, so I am sure I will meet up with you again." He started to pull the cart down the street.

"*Sláinte!*" Theo shouted to Bairre as the trickster disappeared down the road.

What Theo couldn't see was the grin on Bairre's face. The trickster knew he had set his hook, and now he just needed to reel the lad in.

THE O'NEIL

The Copper Tap

Mickey and Kelly finished their surveillance of the Avoca mines from the outside as best they could. They sketched maps of the various buildings, storage areas, and entrances. They passed the information on to the mysterious stranger, the masked rebel. The next step in their plan was to get inside the gates, and for that they needed either to get invited in or to persuade a miner to join the cause.

The Gannon brothers had agreed that they needed some way to prove their credentials as true rebels. They suspected that the miners were tough, hardened men who wouldn't join their cause unless they believed that the brothers were serious players in the rebellion. During the preceding Sunday that they trained with the masked rebel, they decided to "borrow" their guns for the week, thereby breaking a strict rule—that the guns should not ever leave the cave unless the brothers had an authorized specific mission. The brothers justified their "borrowing" in order to prove their credentials as a legitimate mission, and if they were to replace the guns early on the following Sunday, no one would know the better.

Bairre suggested that the guns might help with his recruitment of The O'Neil too. "I have him hooked, and now I just need to reel him in!" Bairre acted out reeling in a fish. His brothers laughed at how ridiculous he looked.

The best place to meet some miners was at a bar just outside the mines. Almost all the miners stopped there for a pint after work. The term *bar* was applied loosely, as it was nothing more than a shack. Mickey wondered what the appeal was for them to visit the place—besides the pints, that is. Nonetheless, he knew that the run-down bar would suit their needs. "Our next step is to mingle and meet some miners. Maybe some would join our cause or at least let us get a man on the inside."

The brothers were excited to take this to the next step. They were actually part of the rebellion now!

Mickey looked at his brothers, his face turning serious. "I already arranged to have an accomplice at the pub. A rather good one too, with a long history of getting the Irish to loosen their tongues."

Kelly's face reddened with anger as he stared at his brother and said, a little louder than he intended, "I thought we were a team. You did that without us?"

Mickey smirked. "Don't worry. I didn't really arrange the spy. He was already there. Once you hear his name, you will understand."

"I doubt that," Kelly replied. "Well, what's the name?"

"Mr. Guinness!"

It took a second for Mickey's answer to penetrate the rather thick skulls of his brothers and travel around inside a bit, but it finally landed. "Aye," said Kelly, "now I get it!" They patted each other's backs, rather pleased that they had figured this out on their own. "You're right! No one is better at opening an Irishman's mouth!"

They all had a good laugh about that. Then they made plans for the next day. They would arrive right after the miners finished working, knowing that many would stop by for a pint or two before heading home.

The bar was called The Copper Tap and was run by an old, retired miner whom everyone referred to as Yellow Pete. Pete had mined his whole life, but eventually, his body had become so broken from this arduous job that he could no longer work the mines. Although his body was broken and he looked much older than he was, his spirit was yet as alive as a wild horse's.

Pete had known that he had to come up with a replacement for his mining job, and his spirit led him to an idea. He waited for the proper day, the summer solstice, and headed toward the mine shacks before sunrise. The shacks had not been used for many years; originally, they had been company housing for the miners. They'd been inadequate then and had only fallen into disrepair even more over the years. On that summer solstice day, Pete moved from shack to shack, looking toward the rising sun. He bent down and peered through the large gaps between the wooden slats in each shack's walls. As the miners arrived for their workday, they thought Pete had finally lost his mind. They couldn't imagine what he was up to.

At one point, Pete jumped up (as best he could) and clicked his heels. He made a beeline to the mine office and confronted the new supervisor. "I want to purchase one of the shacks out there," he declared. "That third one from the right."

The supervisor laughed at him. "Buy it?! Are you mad? It's only good for firewood at this point!" He blew out a breath while rolling his eyes, then looked at Pete in disbelief. "You can have it for free."

Pete chuckled, tipped his cap, and walked toward the door, smiling. Just before stepping out, he turned and said, "I quit!"

The supervisor grabbed a paperweight from his desktop and threw it toward Pete, but the old miner had already slammed the office door tight.

Yellow Pete always had something magical about him. An aura, some called it. Maybe it was just his joviality. Everyone liked him. He had the makings of a perfect bartender. If anyone could transform a shack made of a single layer of wood with large gaps into a bar, it was Yellow Pete.

When his fellow miners heard about his new endeavor, they pointed out the large gaps in the walls and roof and told him that rain would pour in. In Ireland rain was not a rare event, they said. Pete just laughed at their taunts and tapped his head. "My bar also lets in the light! That's what's important. A little rain never hurt anyone in Ireland, for Christ's sake." He looked up at the clouds and scoffed. "If rain melted ye, ye all would be dissolved by now!"

Yellow Pete's bar became a place filled with light, where even enemies drank together without trouble. The most interesting thing about the bar was the light. Even though there were only a few candles and oil lamps inside, anyone coming upon it would note bright light escaping from inside through the gaps in the boards. It seemed, sometimes, that the sun itself was stopping by for a pint. The light was the magic of *An Sconna Copair* ("The Copper Tap")!

Pete had a keg of Guinness Draught and a few bottles of Jameson's Whiskey on the shelf and nothing else. He modified the tap on the keg himself, replacing the standard tap with a chunk of misshapen copper ore that he stole from the mines to manifest the bar's namesake. His happiest moment was nailing the sign "*An Sconna Copair*" above the door. To name his bar, he proudly used the Gaelic, a language outlawed by the English. The name was a poke in the eye to them—a small poke, but a poke nonetheless.

On this day the Gannon brothers walked toward Yellow Pete's bar. They decided that they would avoid using aliases, since some of the miners might recognize who they were. Their shady reputation, they felt, would not be a problem among this group, who likely had their own history of growing up poor in Ireland.

They grabbed a seat at the bar and waited for the bartender to notice them. He was an old man, bent over a sink or counter behind the bar. The bar itself was rather busy, filled with miners in various forms of inebriation, song, and laughter. Eventually, the bartender finished what he was doing and shuffled toward the trio. The brothers then realized that he wasn't just bent over performing a task; he was permanently bent over. He reminded them of a tree on a windy cliff bending toward the sunshine.

"What can I do for ye?"

"We'll each take a Guinness and a shot of Jameson's," Mickey answered.

The old man howled with laughter, revealing a wall of yellow teeth that was missing quite a few bricks. His breath hit them like a tidal wave, telling the brothers that those last few teeth didn't have much time left either. Once he stopped laughing, he said, "That's a fine choice, since that's the only things I serve here!"

They watched him use his forearm to draw the Guinness, as his hands didn't appear to be of much use, due to maybe arthritis or past injuries. His knees didn't seem to be in much better shape either. He winced with every step he took. He shuffled back and forth a few times until he had them set up. "My name is Yellow Pete," he said in a scratchy, breathless voice as he reached out his twisted hand to each of them.

The brothers shook his hand as best they could, and each replied with their names.

"What brings you three into my bar? You don't look like miners."

Mickey had an answer ready: "Well, we are hoping to be miners, as we are between jobs right now. Are they hiring?"

Yellow Pete used his twisted left hand to rub his bristly chin, as if he were polishing Aladdin's lamp to make an answer appear. After a few seconds, he answered, "Well, I don't rightly know, as I have retired from mining. Everyone else in here is a miner, so I think that is your best bet. Talk to them."

Kelly spoke up. "What do the words on the sign above the door mean? It doesn't look like English."

"That's the Gaelic for 'The Copper Tap,' the name I gave this place."

"Isn't Gaelic outlawed in Ireland?"

"Aye." He gave no further comment.

After a few seconds of embarrassed silence, Mickey spoke. "I understand where the name for the bar came from"—he gestured toward the tap—"but where did you get the name Yellow Pete?"

Mickey didn't realize he had just made a mistake, for Yellow Pete had the Irish gift of gab, and this simple question set his mouth meandering through the story of his life. They were anxious to start mingling with the miners to get the information they needed and maybe even a recruit, but they were held fast to their chairs by Pete.

Pete told them that the miners referred to the sulfur they mined as "Devil's Gold" and that he had got his nickname from that sulfur. He'd always been covered in sulfur dust, and he'd always smelled of sulfur. He told them that his work had gotten to a point where his body was broken and where he could barely breathe. He told them he'd always wanted to own a bar and that retiring from the mines had finally given him this opportunity. He felt that bartending was his true calling. He then launched into more mining stories, barely taking a breath between them. As miners came up to the bar, Pete just waved at them, signaling they should serve themselves while he was tied up regaling his new customers with stories.

Around this part of the conversation, the brothers' minds were drifting. Kelly was thinking about a raccoon chewing off his leg to extricate himself from a trap. Mickey and Bairre had to pee so badly that they felt their back teeth were starting to float. After finishing their third round, Kelly finally spoke up: "Excuse us, Pete, but we have to take a piss."

"The outhouse is out the back." Pete tipped his head in that direction.

The three of them jumped off their stools as though they were ablaze and bolted toward the door. When they opened the back door, they were stunned by the vision that greeted them. The landscape was barren, as if the plants had given up trying to grow in this place. What was left was land covered in yellow dust except for a well-worn black path to the outhouse.

They finished their business and stepped back into the bar, careful to take a wide berth around Pete. They split up and began mingling among the groups of miners spread out at the few tables within the place.

As they expected, the Guinness was doing its job. All the miners they spoke with were rather chatty and were happy to answer anything the brothers would ask. They spoke freely about the mines as well as about their hatred of the English.

The brothers occasionally regrouped to inform one another on their progress. "I met a miner nicknamed Cole," Kelly reported, a look of pride on his face. "He seems to be the most promising so far. He not only told me about the mines, but he may be interested in joining us."

"Cole is an unusual name for an Irishman," Bairre stated.

"That's exactly what I said to him. He told me his real first name is

Cathal, but they call him Cole because his last name is Cannon. Irish humor!"

They all got a laugh out of that!

They decided they had done enough for that night. And they agreed that showing off the guns had impressed a lot of the miners. They also felt comfortable that no one would report them. The miners hated the English just as much as the brothers did.

They decided it wouldn't be proper to do an Irish goodbye—leaving a gathering without saying anything—so they nervously approach the bar to say goodbye to Yellow Pete. They felt he could not possibly have any more stories to tell. They were wrong, of course.

They were able to escape a bit quicker than during their last conversation, however, as Pete was looking a little tired. Nevertheless, it was good that they did talk with him some more. He told them that there would be a special event at the bar on the following night. It was likely that every miner would attend. It gave the brothers a perfect opportunity to make more connections.

On most nights The Copper Tap was just a place for hard drinking, joking, and bad singing by the miners. But the next night was to be a bit different. Yellow Pete's niece from Dublin, Saoirse,[10] was visiting. She was known as one of the best fiddle players in all of Ireland. He described Saoirse's voice as one that would make angels weep. The Copper Tap was to have live entertainment for the first time in its existence.

And with that, the brothers thanked Pete and started the walk back to their flat in Wicklow.

Word of Saoirse's performance at The Copper Tap had been spreading among the mine workers for several days already. Nothing could be kept secret from those Irishmen, especially when it came to music. When John first heard the news, it gave him an idea. He had to bring Theo with him to see the show. Not only would it be entertaining for his son, but it would be an important part of Theo's truly understanding Irish history. He knew that the history taught in books was only a bird's eye view. It was

---

10 Pronounced "Sur-shuh."

the history of kings, queens, and warriors. The history taught from the mouth of poets and musicians, on the other hand, was the true history of the people. That history summoned the happiness and sorrow of the common men, women, and children who had built and lived in the country. It was vital that he expose Theo to this story.

John heard that Saoirse performed both classic Irish folk songs as well as original music. John was excited to have a chance to hear her songs. He let Marianne know he would take Theo to the performance after work. Theo would come up to the mines to meet his da, and they would go to The Copper Tap.

On the night of the performance, both John and Theo were giddy with excitement. They stepped into the shack and were greeted by the sight of a raucous crowd of miners and guests. On this night The Copper Tap was supplying the most revered things to many Irishmen: whiskey, laughter, and music (in no particular order).

Saoirse began playing, and the crowd was stunned into silence. The sounds of her fiddle and her voice were as beautiful as anything any of them had ever heard. As the night progressed, the spectators began singing along to the classic folk tunes that they all knew by heart.

During the show, John leaned over to Theo. "Listen to the pauses in her songs. She does those better than anyone I've ever heard. It's during those pauses that you can really understand the song. Watch the crowd right afterward. You will see them dance and sing with even more vigor." He glanced back toward Saoirse before turning once again toward Theo. "Her songs will make you laugh and cry because life makes you laugh and cry, and a folk musician knows how to transform life into notes. Those notes are like breadcrumbs, leading you through the darkness into the light."

A short time into the show, the Gannon brothers sauntered in. They immediately noted the large crowd and were ardently excited by the thought of all the likely recruits into the Irish Republican Brotherhood.

Theo noticed Bairre (aka Wolfe) and leaned over to his da and whispered, "Hey, Wolfe Tone just walked in."

John laughed over Theo's apparent joke. "Surely, he didn't rise from the dead."

"Not the original Wolfe Tone. Just someone I met with the same name."

"Where would he be? I'd like to meet him."

Theo pointed toward the bar. "He's over there near the bar with two other guys."

John recognized the Gannon brothers, was familiar with their reputation, and he could barely keep his composure. "Well, son, that man has been lying to you. He's one of the Gannon brothers from Wicklow. They are nothing but trouble, believe me. I forbid you to talk or associate with them." He leaned in close to make sure he correctly heard everything his son was to say. "Tell me more about what he said to you."

Theo told his da the story of how they'd met and how he'd fixed the man's cart. He went on to say that he'd been encountering him regularly after school because the man's delivery route went down that street, and that he would stop to talk. That he loved to talk about Irish history.

"Did he want anything from you? If I know the Gannon brothers' reputation, they always have an angle or a deceitful scheme."

"Well, he claims to be a part of the new Irish Brotherhood, and they plan to free Ireland from English rule. He thought I might be interested in joining the cause."

John's head nearly exploded with anger. He could picture Theo innocently being drawn into a disastrous endeavor. He could see him being marched off to some English prison or, even worse, winding up dead. "Well, I will have a little chat with the Gannons. I promise that they won't bother you again."

John tried his best to calm down and get his mind back into the music, but his thoughts remained on Theo and the Gannons. He nonetheless put on a neutral facade for Theo, so the lad could hear the words and music of the real Ireland.

When they arrived home, Theo went to bed. Marianne immediately saw that John was upset by something. "What's wrong, *mo gra*? Didn't you enjoy the music?"

"The music was wonderful. Saoirse has the voice of an angel, and I didn't know the fiddle could be played that well."

They both sat down near the fireplace, and John told Marianne what he was upset about.

"Theo is just an adolescent," Marianne said. "He could easily be tricked into joining their lost cause." She reached out and took John's hand. "Oh, John, I am worried. I don't want Theo to fall in with the likes of them."

"Aye, those brothers are nothing but trouble. I am going to pay them a visit first thing tomorrow morning and put a stop to this right now. I will leave early for work." He looked toward Marianne barely able to control the anger building inside. "Theo can walk himself to school. Just tell him I had some early business to finish in Wicklow."

They stood, embraced, and walked toward their bedroom. Both were worried about what any involvement with the Gannon brothers, however superficial, might bring to their door. Neither of them slept very well that night.

The Flat

John woke early and walked off toward Wicklow, carrying a heavy rage. His thoughts were occupied by the future of his son, Theo. Before he had left The Copper Tap the night before, he had obtained the Gannons' address from one of the miners he knew who often crossed paths with the brothers. The results of not one of the path-crossing experiences had been good either.

At about the same time, Mickey awoke with a terrible headache in the flat of the miner Cole. He had left The Copper Tap with him, and they had continued drinking into the wee sma' hours of the morning. He quietly rose from the couch and left with an Irish goodbye. Heading home toward his flat, he was in good spirits despite his aching head. He had persuaded Cole to agree to join the Brotherhood, and he knew this would very much please the masked stranger.

John reached the Gannons' flat, and his anger exploded into a pounding on their door. Bairre woke with a start, but he quickly calmed down when he remembered that Mickey had not made it home from the pub the night before. Surely, that pounding had to be him playing a prank. As Bairre opened the door, he started to say, "Jaysus, Mickey, you'll awaken the dead—"

He never finished his sentence because John reached in, grabbed a handful of his shirt, lifted him off the floor, and ran him into the far wall. "You bastard!" John yelled.

The commotion woke Kelly, who appeared suddenly from around a doorway. John reacted instantly with a strong kick into his gut. The force knocked him into the perpendicular wall as well as knocked the wind out of him. John dragged Bairre over toward Kelly and threw him down. "Now we are going to have a little chat." He stood menacingly above them and asked in a loud voice, "Where's your brother Mickey? I need him to hear this too."

Kelly, having recovered his breath, replied, "He isn't here. He never made it home from The Copper Tap."

"Well, you two can give him my message."

John never got to give him his message, because just at that moment, the police burst through the door. "Hands up! It looks like we've finally got you infamous Gannon brothers, once and for all!"

John turned around, raised his hands, then started to say, "You're mistaken."

"Shut your mouth," the sergeant yelled as he slugged John across the face with his billy club, knocking him to the floor. The other officers ran forward and quickly cuffed the three men's hands behind their backs, and got them up into a kneeling position facing the wall.

John, stunned from the hit, didn't resist, but he started to plead for the officers to listen to him. He was trying to explain who he was and why he was there.

"Put a gag on that one," the sergeant said, snarling. "I am sick of hearing his voice."

John was gagged by one of the officers.

"Now," the sergeant addressed the captives, "we had a spy tell us that you three have graduated from being worthless petty criminals into something much worse. Traitors to the Crown!" He produced a paper from his uniform coat and cackled as he waved it at the back of the three men's heads facing the wall. "What I have here is a warrant to search this place for evidence of your treason." He threw the warrant down on the floor as his hatred for these traitors did not permit him to hand it to them. "If we find that evidence, your careers will come to a sudden end."

The officers began searching the flat, making sure to break and scatter anything they touched. It took them only a few minutes to find the Colt revolvers under the sink, the very guns the masked Brotherhood stranger had insisted should remain at the cave unless the brothers were on a legitimate mission.

"Well, look what we found!" The sergeant, grinning in delight, clicked his tongue. "I think that's all the evidence that we need." He pointed toward the courtyard. "Take them out back!"

John struggled to speak. He needed to explain that he was no traitor. This was just a mistake of being in the wrong place at the wrong time. He was not a Gannon brother. The gag, unfortunately, was very effective.

Mickey, meanwhile, came upon the scene. Seeing the police wagon in front of the flat, the wagon's team of four horses impatiently pawing at the street, he knew there was big trouble. He slipped between the buildings across the street to observe unseen.

John, Kelly, and Bairre were made to kneel in the courtyard facing away from the building. The sergeant started to read the charges against them. John, trapped in a nightmare, struggled to make them understand his innocence, but he couldn't form intelligible words through the gag.

The sergeant finished with their sentences: "You are hereby sentenced to death as traitors to the Crown."

A feeling of hopelessness washed over John. He took one last look up at the blue sky above and noted only one cloud. The pig was smirking at him. He couldn't help but laugh, despite his current situation. He then bowed his head to see one last time the soil of his beloved Ireland and filled his head with memories of Marianne and Theo. Just before the bullet left the gun, he whispered, "*Is brea liom tu.*"[11]

John fell face down into the arms of his beloved Ireland. The medallion around his neck swung around and settled on his back, between his shoulder blades. He had always tried to grow toward the light, but sometimes the light bends farther away.

---

[11] "I love you."

Mickey, across the street, heard the report of the rifles. *POP, POP, POP.* He knew exactly what the sounds were, although he was confused that he had heard three shots rather than two. He realized that his brothers' lives had just ended that morning, and he choked back tears as he resisted the urge to run to them.

Meanwhile, behind the flat, the sergeant shouted another command: "Search their bodies!"

They found nothing surprising on the Gannon brothers, but one of the officers turned to his sergeant, holding an Avoca mines identity card he had retrieved from John's body. "Sir, this one may not be a Gannon. The card he had says his name is John O'Neil. He was a miner."

The sergeant took the card, read the name, and scratched his head. "Our spy never mentioned this name. Their network may be bigger than we'd thought. We may have inadvertently found another conspirator. Let's get back to the station and find out more about this John O'Neil."

As they were about to leave, the sergeant pointed to the three bodies. "Call the gravediggers to come and take these traitors to the paupers' grave and bury them there, unmarked. That's all they deserve!"

The police left the flat with the confiscated guns and piled into the wagon. The sergeant flicked his crop at the horses, and the wagon pulled away. Mickey gave them plenty of time to make sure they were a good distance away before he came out of hiding. He ran into the flat and out to the courtyard. He was shocked to see three bodies lying prone with hands cuffed behind their backs. He sobbed, and he said his last goodbyes to Kelly and Bairre. Then he moved on to the third body. This man was gagged. There was some kind of medallion on his back. Mickey recognized the man as John O'Neil, one of the miners at the Avoca mines. He found nothing on him except the medallion. He took it and put it in his pocket.

Mickey knew he didn't have much time. The police must have mistaken John O'Neil for *him*. If they realized their mistake, they would never admit it; they would claim O'Neil was one of the traitors too, and then they would look for his friends and family to widen the net they cast. Once they figured out where O'Neil lived, they would show up there, looking for more weapons. And only God knows what else they would do. Whatever the case, the tragedy that had befallen John O'Neil and soon no doubt his wife might be the spark that would convince the adolescent son, The O'Neil, the one whom Bairre had been working to recruit, to join the Brotherhood out of revenge.

Mickey knew where the lad lived, thanks to Bairre's good work. He ran down the road toward the O'Neils' cottage, the medallion in his pocket, hoping he would get there in time.

After Marianne had seen Theo off on his way to school, she was cleaning up after the breakfast and mopping the floor. Now she saw a man running toward the cottage. From a distance she thought it first to be John, returning home for some reason. As he got closer, though, she realized the man wasn't John. She dried her hands on a towel and opened the door. She stood firmly on the threshold, arms akimbo.

As the stranger approached, he slowed down and said breathlessly, "Ma'am, my name is Mickey Gannon, and I have important news."

Marianne just stood there silently and stared him down. She knew all about Mickey Gannon and his criminal activities from what John had told her just the night before. She knew his presence could mean only trouble.

"The constables raided our flat this morning," Mickey continued. "They found guns there, and they executed my two brothers."

"Why are you telling me this? It has nothing to do with me." Nevertheless, Marianne felt an anxiety growing within her.

"Ma'am, I am sorry to tell you that I think they mistook your husband for me. They killed him too."

Marianne's heart felt like it had turned to dust. The dread started there and spread through her body. "You're lying! I've heard about you! You are nothing but a swindler, and this must be some trap you're setting for me."

Mickey reached into his pocket, slowly lifted the medallion out, and offered it to her. "I knew you wouldn't believe me. That's why I brought this."

Marianne immediately realized that John would never have let this scoundrel take his medallion unless he was truly dead. As she took the medallion and pressed it to her chest, tears streamed down her cheeks.

"I've come to give you that news," Mickey continued, "but also a warning. Once they figure out who your husband is and where he lives, the police will surely come for you. It won't take them long." He looked over her shoulder, both for emphasis as well as to see if the police were coming down the road. "Rather than to admit they made a mistake, they will just claim he was working with us. A traitor to the Crown." Mickey began to sweat, wondering if he would ever get through to her. "They will seek out anyone associated with him. You need to run and hide."

Marianne's sorrow suddenly turned to a steely anger. She was sick of dealing with the politics of Ireland. It caught everyone in its net, no matter their innocence. "I will not leave my home. I am innocent. As was John."

Mickey was blunt. "His innocence didn't matter to his executioners, and neither will yours or your son's."

At the mention of Theo, thoughts rapidly formed in Marianne's mind. She played all the different imagined situations that might result from this day. Only one situation guaranteed Theo's safety and freedom. "You need to assist me now!" she declared.

Mickey was taken aback by her sudden change in demeanor and even more so when she grabbed a handful of his shirt and pulled him into the cottage. He stumbled and fell, coming to rest near the hearth. As he got his bearings, he spoke, "They will be here any minute. We must leave now, or we will both be either dead or locked up. I know just the place to hide you too."

"This is my home, and I will not flee from those brutes who killed my John. Before I let you leave, you are going to help me clean out this cottage of any evidence of the existence of my son," she commanded, while hoping that the Jesuit had never filed Theo's baptismal certificate.

The pair went through the cottage, filling a large sack as they went. They stuffed it with Theo's clothes, old toys, and sundry other things that suggested that John and Marianne had a son. Marianne made sure to include John's cap into the sack, so that Theo would have something of his da to remember him by. With the job complete, Marianne released Mickey, who quickly fled into the wooded hills, carrying the sack. Marianne's final instruction to him was to intercept her son from school and to keep him safely hidden until she cleared up this mess. She was a logical person and felt she could convince the police of their innocence. She even felt she had the upper hand, given that the police had killed an innocent man.

The police, however, did not work by logic. They worked by orders and emotions. They did arrive a short time later, as Mickey had predicted. The sergeant stepped up to the cottage with Marianne standing defiantly in the doorway. He handed her a paper and said, "I have a warrant to search these premises. Step aside!"

Marianne didn't move an inch but stared daggers at him. The sergeant just shoved her into the cottage and yelled to his men, "Search the place, and don't leave even a crumb undisturbed."

His men invaded the cottage and began to ransack it. They followed orders perfectly, disrupting and breaking as much as possible. Marianne stood silently, stoned-faced. She would not give them the benefit of seeing her weep.

When there was nothing left to search, the sergeant stepped up to Marianne. "We know that John O'Neil, your spouse, lived here. We also know that he was working with the rebellion against the Crown."

"That's a lie!" Marianne screamed. "He had nothing to do with those scoundrels!"

"Well, he was found with those rebels," the sergeant replied with a smirk, "and they possessed illegal weapons."

Marianne could tell the sergeant was enjoying this, and she was powerless against him. She realized that if she told him the reason for John's visit to the Gannons' flat, the existence of Theo would be revealed. She held onto the hope that they didn't know about their son. Maybe the Jesuit, Father Bolger, had known better than to file the baptismal certificate. It was better to be a ghost when one was Irish in Ireland. Thank God for the Jesuits. "You did your search, now leave me be!"

The sergeant gave another smirk. "Oh wait, what is this? I almost forgot I have another warrant here." He went through the motions of patting his coat, as if looking for something. "Ah, here it is." He handed another paper to Marianne.

As she began reading the warrant, the sergeant said, "You, Marianne O'Neil, are under arrest for treason against the Crown."

Marianne couldn't believe what was happening. Their quiet, happy life was being shattered by the English government. She remained speechless as the officers put her in handcuffs and marched her toward the police wagon.

The sergeant continued, "You will be taken to Dublin Castle, where you will be interrogated and incarcerated while awaiting your sentence." He shook his finger at her in a scolding manner. "And if you are hiding weapons on these grounds, we will surely find them!"

Marianne still held on to the hope that she could clear this up once in Dublin. She imagined being reunited with Theo and returning to their cottage to live out their years in peace. Together, maybe, they could overcome the loss of John.

As the wagon carrying Marianne to Dublin disappeared down the road, one of the officers turned to the sergeant and asked, "What do we do with the cottage?"

The sergeant replied enthusiastically, "Call the explosives team and have them blow it to pieces!"

"But sir, won't she be coming back?"

The sergeant laughed vigorously, then replied, "Believe me, I know how Dublin works in these matters. She won't be coming back."

Mickey stayed hidden in the woods before leaving for Wicklow. He observed the police arrival and Marianne being taken away. He knew where she was likely headed. He needed to be able to tell The O'Neil what had transpired there. Once he saw her taken away, he grabbed the sack and headed toward the cave. He would hide the lad's belongings and then head to Wicklow to intercept him. He would keep his word—but not out of kindness, more out of getting a recruit into the Brotherhood.

Mickey knew from his training that Marianne was going to be interrogated in Dublin. The masked stranger had told them that if they were ever caught alive, that's where they would end up. He'd also warned them that it might be better to be dead than to be taken to Dublin Castle. Either way, he'd told them, you would never see Wicklow again.

Mickey hid near the school and waited. He didn't want to be recognized on the streets of Wicklow. Once he saw the lad coming toward him, he stepped out, tipped his cap, and said, "Hello, are you the lad they call The O'Neil?"

"Aye, sir, I am, for that is my name." A brief look of confusion appeared on his face before it dissolved and he said, "I recognize you from The Copper Tap. You're one of the Gannon brothers."

"Aye, I am Mickey Gannon." He stuck out his hand to shake Theo's.

"Then, there's a problem, sir. My da instructed me that I was never to talk or associate with any of ye. He said you would be a bad influence."

"We do have that reputation, but things have changed. We are now only committed to the fight for Irish freedom and have given up on everything else."

Theo had no reply. He remembered the brother who had falsely called himself Wolfe. He really liked him and supported Irish freedom, but he wasn't sure about trusting a Gannon again.

"Listen, lad, I was instructed by your mother to walk you home directly today. She did not want you to meet your father at the mines. I have much to tell you on the way." He tried to walk alongside the lad, but Theo shied away, still untrusting. "I swear that your ma asked me to do that today."

Theo shrugged, then followed a few steps behind Mickey so he could keep an eye on him. He wondered if he was making the best choice.

As they walked, Mickey told the lad about the rebel training and activities. He told him how his brothers had died that very morning, fighting for Irish freedom.

Theo became absorbed in the story as Mickey spoke of the heroics of the rebellion. Gradually, he sped up, to walk by Mickey's side. "I am sorry for you, Mickey," he said in a hushed tone. "The loss of your brothers must be a painful cross to bear."

"They died for Ireland, so I couldn't be prouder of them." Mickey timed breaking the news to Theo about his own loss until they could see the cottage from the woods. Then he turned toward the lad. "Your ma sent me to you, to protect you from the police."

"I don't understand," Theo replied with a wrinkled brow.

Mickey pointed toward the cottage in the distance. "Look!"

Theo focused on the cottage and now saw a police wagon and several policemen scurrying around their cottage.

"Let's sit down, and I will explain." Mickey guided Theo to sit next to him on a log. "The constables got a report that your parents were involved with rebel activities."

Theo gave a nervous laugh. "That's a false accusation!"

"Yes, but that is all it takes in Ireland today."

"But once they search the cottage and find nothing, I am sure everything will be fine," Theo said with a shake in his voice.

"Unfortunately, you are wrong. They've already arrested your ma. I saw them taking her away in handcuffs, probably to Dublin to be interrogated." He shook his head as if to reinforce that what he was saying was true. "I watched them right from this spot."

Theo felt his heart pounding in his chest, and his mind filled with a confused anger. "My da would not let that happen!"

Mickey looked the lad in the eyes and said flatly, "They executed him as a traitor and took his body to be buried in an unmarked pauper's grave."

Theo instantly stood and ran toward the cottage. Mickey was caught off guard for a second but then bolted off behind the lad. "Lad, stop, if they see you, you'll be taken too!"

Although Mickey ran as fast as he could, the lad was just too fast. Theo nearly made it to the edge of the woods when they were both knocked down by the blast.

As they struggled to their feet, Theo realized where the blast had come from. The cottage was gone. There was just a white cloud rising toward the sky. A cloud filled with the memories of his childhood, his parents, and the life they had lived together.

In silence Theo watched the cloud drift away. The explosion had taken away whatever Theo had been. He was no longer that person, he had become someone else. His soul darkened, and his spine steeled. Theo now knew that Mickey was telling the truth, without a doubt. He turned toward Mickey. "I want to join the Brotherhood."

Mickey felt a chill go up his back. The lad did not shed a single tear, but he stared so deeply that it made Mickey fearful of him.

He reached out his hand to The O'Neil. "Welcome to the Brotherhood. We will avenge your father's death and see what we can do to get your ma freed."

Then the pair walked off silently toward the cave.

THE O'NEIL

The Chemist

The O'Neil's shadow led the way into the cave until it dissolved into darkness. The bright sun warmed The O'Neil's back, but he neither felt its warmth nor noticed its light. He walked determined and driven by anger and lust for revenge. His arms bounced off the sharp edges of the tunnel as pieces of rock crumbled from the force of his anger. It was a journey of a thousand cuts, a self-flagellation. He transiently replaced his intense mental pain with the pain of the body.

He had arrived at the cavern, and he surveyed his new home, where the day turned to night, clean air to dust, and warm blood to ice. In the cavernous center, if he had turned and looked just to his right, he would have seen a small flicker of light from the entrance. He cared not to see it, though, for he had left the light of his past somewhere outside his cave.

In the center of the cavern The O'Neil placed his school bag, then he paced, pounding his right fist into his left palm. The blood dripping down from his cut arms smeared across his palm. He mumbled as the thousand thoughts firing through his mind, no longer contained, slipped through his lips.

"Listen, lad, I know you're hurting and angry, but we need to lie low for a while."

"My name is The O'Neil, and you will refer to me by that name," The O'Neil stated as he stepped up face to face with Mickey. "I am not your lad!"

Mickey shivered from a stare that was both feral and dangerous. Even in the dim light of the oil lamps, he could see a darkness in The O'Neil's eyes. The O'Neil also felt this inner darkness and wondered if the light of his da would ever find him again.

Mickey broke the uncomfortable silence. "We will find out where they took your ma. Maybe we can even get word to her that you are safe."

"How will you do that?" The O'Neil asked skeptically.

"Oh, lad—I mean, The O'Neil—we have the eyes and ears of the entirety of Ireland. The Brotherhood is everywhere. In the meantime, we will find you a place to live."

"Don't bother," he replied as he gestured around the cave with his bloody hands. "I am going to live right here until my ma is released."

Lining the walls of the cave were various crates of sulfur, saltpeter, charcoal, and recycled bullet shells. He also noted various tools, which let him know exactly what task he was to be assigned.

"Suit yourself, but this is not the most comfortable quarters."

The O'Neil had no reply but just started to unpack his belongings from the sack that Mickey had earlier brought to the cave.

Mickey had to stay with The O'Neil for now, as he could never return to his flat in Wicklow. They would have to wait for the masked stranger's next visit. Then they would find out about their new living situation, as well as more about The O'Neil's ma.

Mickey snuck into town to procure some food. The O'Neil stayed behind, flatly refusing to leave the cave. There was plenty of water from a nearby mountain spring. There was also a kiln that could double as a stove.

The O'Neil was mostly silent when the two were together, only speaking when necessary. The silence made Mickey nervous, his imagination filling in the silence with what he suspected The O'Neil might be contemplating. He wondered how much The O'Neil blamed him for his da's execution and whether he was considering that revenge was in order.

The masked stranger arrived as expected on Sunday. He started right in on Mickey, "You *eejit*! I should take you outside right now and put a bullet between your eyes! You nearly blew our whole operation here!"

Mickey, flustered, responded, "So, you know what happened?"

"Of course! We watched the whole thing unfold. You know we have eyes everywhere. We also noted that you lost weapons and comrades and that you caused an innocent life to be lost."

Mickey tried to shift blame to his brothers. "It was my *eejit* brothers. If I had known that they took the weapons from the cave, I would have stopped them."

"We still blame you as well." He poked his finger firmly into Mickey's chest. "You should have been more observant."

Mickey, fearful for his life, avoided eye contact and just looked down toward the ground.

The masked stranger continued, still poking at his chest for emphasis. "You are also responsible for replacing two comrades."

Mickey, seeing a glimmer of hope for his life to be spared, nodded toward The O'Neil. "This one here might be worth two. He has agreed to join the cause." He shuffled his feet to relieve his building anxiety. "And I've also signed on a miner name Cole."

Ignoring Mickey, the masked stranger turned toward The O'Neil, looked him over, and then asked, "Is that true?"

"Aye."

"And what is it you can offer the Brotherhood and Ireland?" he asked, pretending to not already know.

The O'Neil pointed to the crates along the walls. "Looks to me like you need someone to put these to good use."

"You can do that?" The masked stranger feigned surprise.

"Aye" was The O'Neil's simple reply.

The masked stranger turned again toward Mickey and, with a straight face, lied to him: "If that's true and he can do a right job, you may have made up for your stupidity." He then turned back to The O'Neil. "You have a week to prove your worth. I will return next Sunday to see what you have accomplished." He looked The O'Neil in the eyes and said with finality: "If I am satisfied, then you're in." As he turned to leave, he again addressed Mickey: "Follow me. We have a place for you to stay, but we need to keep you *underground* for a while longer." As the two walked toward the cave entrance, the masked stranger turned his head and said over his shoulder to The O'Neil, "I will find out about your ma and bring you news about her next Sunday on my return. You have my word."

The O'Neil, now alone, first developed a routine. He knew he needed to stay healthy and busy, lest the demons in his mind take over. He woke each day before dawn and ran along various mountain paths around the cave. He ran until his legs could take no more. He started small campfires to cook; he avoided using the kiln, for he had other plans for that.

He spent the days of his first full week creating a list of the things he would need in order to complete his assigned task and to improve the safety and comfort of his new home. He would present the list to the masked stranger as a requirement for his working for the Brotherhood.

Then he set about mixing up his own formula for gunpowder. He had an idea to increase the force and velocity of his bullets. His chemistry training made him meticulous in his measurements. He had to repair and rebalance the scale available in the cave, as it was not in the best shape when he found it.

He worked in near darkness, careful to use only a lamp near the cave entrance tunnel, to avoid the danger of explosion or fire. He was not satisfied with the safety of his workspace ventilation. He added safety lamps and mirrors to his list for the masked stranger.

He worked for hours each day, repeatedly measuring and filling the recycled shells, packing each carefully and setting them aside to await their metal crowns. Into each cartridge he added a little bit of his anger. He imagined the amount of that anger equal to the grams of gunpowder that went into each shell. He also imagined that with each shell he packed his anger would lessen by an equivalent amount. As time went on, he realized that this was not an effective therapy, as his anger had only grown by the end of the first week. Each morning he seemed to push himself even harder, fueled by a desire to control his anger.

When he got bored of packing bullets, he moved on to working on larger explosives. He would wait for safer conditions to mix ingredients, but he could still safely work on design, timers, and fuses.

When Sunday arrived, so did the masked stranger. Mickey was nowhere to be seen. The O'Neil wondered just briefly what had happened to Mickey, but he really didn't care enough to ask. He figured that Mickey Gannon might have become one of "the disappeared."

The O'Neil responded to the masked stranger's greeting with only an outstretched hand holding a list of the supplies he needed.

The masked stranger looked over the list, nodding as he mentally checked off each of the various items. He seemed to hover over a few items a bit longer than the others, then he spoke with derision: "Most of these make sense, but I don't understand a few items, like copper and fertilizer. What are those for?" His thrusted index finger tapped on the word *fertilizer* in the list. "For Christ's sake, are you planning on growing vegetables up here?"

"You'll understand in due time," The O'Neil stated firmly. "Just get me those items."

The masked stranger ignored his tone and walked along the walls of the cave. "You've been busy."

"Aye."

"I noticed that you neglected to melt down lead for the bullets. I don't understand why, as you have plenty of lead, the molds, and the kiln." He handled a piece of lead and extended it toward The O'Neil's face. "Any reason for that?"

"I need copper first."

"Why the feck do you need copper? Bullets are made from lead!" He stepped up toward The O'Neil. "You're not turning yellow on us, are you?"

"I am going to make a better bullet design. Ones that will have better velocity and penetration ability. I am going to give the lead a copper jacket." With his hands he mimicked wrapping an imaginary bullet. "These bullets will perform better than anything the peelers have ever seen." Intrigued, the masked stranger waited to hear more. The O'Neil grinned, undisturbed by the other's skepticism. "Let me explain."

"I am all ears, but this better be good."

"Lead is soft and expands when it hits a target. That expansion reduces some of its energy. Lead is useless against any hard targets, even targets as soft as wood, but especially against buildings." He smiled, knowing that the masked stranger was unlikely to understand such a concept. "I am going to give the bullets an outer coat of copper, a stronger metal. This will prevent so much expansion, and the bullets will have much greater penetration."

The O'Neil knew there was plenty of copper nearby, for he had helped his da mine it. He didn't mention to the stranger that although his idea was scientifically sound, he also wanted a little bit of the copper his da had mined in every bullet fired for Ireland. He also didn't mention that these bullets were less lethal to humans, since they passed through the body rather than expanding and shredding a wide path through flesh. Maybe The O'Neil still hung on to a little bit of the light of his parents and the past.

"I will bring this to our commanders and return next week with their reply, along with the supplies that they agree to provide."

"If they don't agree to my terms, tell them I will just walk away."

The masked stranger laughed vigorously before saying, "No one can just leave. Once you're in, you're in for life. We don't let anyone just leave. You already know too much about our operation." He stared at The O'Neil, who knew exactly what he meant but just steadily returned the stare. "Just ask your friend Mickey, although I doubt you'd be able to find him."

The O'Neil, expressionless, replied, "He was no friend of mine." With that he turned his back on the masked stranger, signaling the end of their conversation. After folding The O'Neil's list into his pocket, the masked stranger left the cave.

The O'Neil spent the next week preparing for his job. The priority was the safety of his workspace. He was shocked at how lackadaisically it had been set up. He took advantage of some of the smaller caves nearby to move the explosive materials. The kiln, which was too heavy to move that far, would remain in the bigger cave. He was not completely happy with that setup, worried about toxic fumes. He was able to move the kiln closer to the entrance, though, using logs to roll it and wooden sticks as levers. That would at least improve ventilation somewhat. The smaller caves were brighter, negating a need for oil lamps, something he did not want anywhere near gunpowder. His most challenging task was fashioning new molds that would enable him to make the copper-jacketed bullets.

He was happy to have some of his books with him, those he had carried home from school on the day his da was killed and his mother arrested. He used the chemistry book to come up with an idea of how to make explosives from fertilizer, which would be much less suspicious to obtain than dynamite. He worked out various "recipes" to test before moving forward with the best one. He continued to work on timer and fuse designs, and in whatever free time he had, he packed more cartridges.

Sunday arrived with the masked stranger bearing gifts. He brought a bed roll, fuel for the lamps and kiln, food, and a small supply of copper, along with the other items that The O'Neil had requested. "This is all the copper I could carry. More will be dropped off in the tunnel throughout the week." He looked around the cave. "I see you reorganized things."

"I had to. The way it was set up before was likely to cause an explosion." The O'Neil gave the masked stranger a condescending look as he gestured about the cave. "I was the most likely victim, so just call it self-preservation."

"I need to let you know about your ma. We did get word to her that you were safe, but the rest of the news is not good. There was a ship sailing to Australia a few days after her arrest, so they did a quick trial and judgment. It was really nothing more than a formality. They already concluded she was guilty. Of course, she denied having anything to do with the Brotherhood and the rebels. The authorities considered her recalcitrance to be a failure of admitting guilt, a failure for atoning for what they were convinced she'd done, so they sentenced her to ten years in a penal colony in Australia, never able to return to Ireland. She will not be able to write or receive communications from Ireland while in the penal colony either." He placed his arm on The O'Neil's shoulder and said, "I am sorry."

The masked stranger awaited some sort of response from The O'Neil, but he remained stone-faced, folding all his anger inside himself. After a moment, he pointed toward various items in the cave. "Then I will keep reminding the English about her until her release, using these. I will not forget her, and I will not let them forget her either."

The O'Neil handed the masked stranger another list of needed supplies and turned back to his work. The stranger nodded, turned, and walked back up the tunnel.

The O'Neil buried himself in his work. His morning workouts continued to increase in intensity, as did his strength and stamina. He continued to perfect his dark craft, aided by his knowledge of chemistry. He focused on creating his copper-jacketed bullets, setting that as his priority. When he was finally satisfied that they were ready, he reported this fact to the masked stranger. They took some out to the firing range near the cave to test them. They both were impressed by their accuracy and penetration ability when tested against various metals and woods. The masked stranger knew that his superiors in the Brotherhood would also be impressed.

The O'Neil began manufacturing these bullets at a frenzied pace. When he had enough for a day, he moved on to working on the explosives, wicks, and timers. He never rested, afraid that his idle mind would recall too much pain.

The bullets and explosives made their way throughout Ireland. The English authorities recognized the similarity and quality of the weapons used in various attacks. They began a determined effort to learn just who was responsible for these high-quality munitions. They began to refer to this unknown person as "the Chemist." The Irish people knew him as

"The O'Neil," although they had no idea of the true identity of the man behind the moniker.

The English authorities seemed incapable of tracking "the Chemist." At any rate, he seemed not to exist in any records they possessed. The O'Neil, from his own perspective, did not really exist any longer either. He was not The O'Neil of his past. He had become someone else. He was a ghost or, better yet, a hermit living in a dark cave. He planned to exile himself from the world for at least the next ten years, ignoring or denying the violence his work was supporting. He just did not care. The only emotion he could feel was anger, and it was not abating over time.

The English authorities became more obsessed with identifying and finding "the Chemist." They could not precisely determine a likely location, since his handiwork was spread widely throughout Ireland. The only human contact he had was the masked stranger. Rebels who were captured, even under torture, gave up no information that was of use to the English. When questioned, the prisoners had all been instructed to use the English term for him, "the Chemist." None of them knew his real identity or his location, so there was really nothing for them to give up. The rebels also knew that if they were to mention his name, The O'Neil, they would receive a punishment of death or worse from their own. The O'Neil was too valuable for them to lose.

Over the ten years' time, The O'Neil changed dramatically, both physically and mentally. He was tall like his da had been, but now he was more muscular and stronger, and he also had a dark, bushy beard.

The O'Neil began to have second thoughts about the violence he was creating. It was those thoughts that had him don his da's cap—the cap his ma had included in the sack of his belongings—and go to Wicklow. It was a risk. There were people in Wicklow who knew both him and his family, and they might recognize him. He felt it unlikely, however, since he now looked nothing like the lad of his childhood. The Brotherhood had also spread word throughout Wicklow that The O'Neil had been exiled along with his ma, which was a story that everyone accepted. They believed that "The O'Neil" was now just a code name in honor of the O'Neil family.

It was a beautiful, soft day with the prevailing mist creating an ethereal ambience. The O'Neil felt like he was walking through a dream.

As he descended the mountain trail, the mist began to clear. He arrived in town under blue skies and clear vision. As he walked around town, he pulled his coat tighter and his cap down low, hiding as much of his face as possible.

He had no plan. He was not sure what propelled him to leave his self-imposed isolation. He wandered aimlessly, avoiding people as much as possible. He eventually found himself walking toward a young lad. As he got closer, he could see that the lad was wearing a newsboy cap and held aloft a newspaper. The boy had slung across his chest a sack filled with newspapers. The O'Neil stopped a short distance away from the lad, to listen to what he was shouting: "Two innocents killed in bombing near Dublin. The Brotherhood blamed!"

The O'Neil felt a stab deep in his soul. He wanted to find out more, but he didn't know if he could face what he already suspected. He approached the lad, holding out a coin for him. "Laddie, I want to buy one of those."

The lad handed him a paper as he took the coin, gulping in fear at the appearance and size of The O'Neil, and without a word turned from him and walked farther down the street.

The O'Neil tucked the paper under his arm without looking at it and walked back toward the wooded path. He'd had enough of reality for this day; he preferred the protection and isolated life of his cave. Reality, however, was tucked under his arm, it was coming to his cave, and he knew it.

The Medallion

The O'Neil stepped back into the darkness of the cave, the outside world tucked under his left arm. The path forward dark, the path backward full of light and memories. He sat in the cavern between both worlds but facing toward the glimmer of light coming from the entrance. On that cold ground he read the newspaper and started to understand his own hatred and the redness that had overtaken his life.

As he read further, he cried for the first time in his memory. He remembered the past and his parents. He remembered the light as it gradually filled the darkness again. He glanced around the cave and began to despise it. His soul started to fill with this light, which gave him the strength to leave the cave and the Brotherhood, despite the consequences. He left the cave with no idea where to go or how to live again. He walked into his new future, knowing it was time.

He knew at that moment he had become a wanted man. If he stayed in Ireland, both the English and now the Brotherhood would continue to search for him. He knew that eventually one of them would succeed. He wandered through the woods toward Wicklow, his da's voice in his head telling him that staying in the light always came with a price. Some would look at the price and refuse to pay, whereas others would agree that the price was worth it. He was among the latter. It was the cost of all things beautiful: the light, his past childhood, his ma, his da, and even himself.

As he walked along, he finally realized where he needed to go. He needed Father Doran. He needed the Jesuit. He walked toward him, the only light he knew still existed.

His beard, heavy on his face, pulled his chin down toward the ground. He smiled at the ants scurrying across the path. Their life of the simplicity of the crumbs, oblivious to the world of humans. Oblivious to the world's hatred, revenge, and greed. He wondered if such a way of living were possible for any man, or was such a life a secret only in the realm of the ants. He made sure to step around the little creatures, not wanting to crush them as they searched for their next crumb, as he continued his path toward happiness again.

He slipped quietly into the church next to his former school. It was peaceful, lit only by candles. He walked over to the confessional, walked in, and closed the door behind him. He kneeled and silently began to pray. As he did, the screen in front of him shushed open.

"Theo, you've returned."

"Aye, Father. I need to confess." Theo was not surprised that Father Doran somehow knew exactly who had stepped into the confessional.

"Continue then."

Theo made the sign of the cross. "Bless me, Father, for I have sinned…"

When Theo finished his confession, he waited. He expected anger and disappointment from Father Doran, but instead he heard only love, support, and forgiveness.

"Theo, I am not giving you Hail Marys for penance." Father Doran leaned in closer toward the screen separating them. "I think there is a much better penance."

Theo held his breath involuntarily as he awaited his fate.

"You need to leave the Brotherhood forever." The priest's voice was stern.

"Father, you are giving me a death sentence for my penance then. No one can leave the Brotherhood. That's why I came to you for help and forgiveness." Theo inhaled, chewed his lip, and nodded. "I have made up my mind already to leave. But how?"

"I would never give a death sentence to anyone. I have many powerful friends who can help you. There is a secret group of wealthy Irish citizens, many Protestants, who are dedicated to freeing Ireland from English rule. Unlike the Brotherhood, though, they are committed to using only peaceful and political means to achieve their goal." He leaned toward the screen between them and whispered. "I am part of that group. Helping you to leave the Brotherhood would for us be a step away from this country's violence and a step toward peace and freedom."

Theo was silent for a minute, trying to hold back tears. Once he had better control of his emotions, he said, "Why would anyone, including you, want to help me after all I've done?"

"I am God's representative on Earth, and His forgiveness is limitless." Tears welled into Theo's eyes, invisible to the priest behind the confessional screen. "As for the group I work with, we understand the predicament of the Irish people. We understand why there is evil on both sides." He nodded sadly in the darkness of the booth. "We are a practical, goal-oriented group, and we are willing to move forward as long as it takes us closer to peace and freedom."

Theo didn't have words to respond. He felt unworthy of their help.

Father Doran continued, "You can stay here for now while I arrange for you to leave Ireland."

"Leave Ireland?"

"Aye, Theo, I am afraid that is the only way. Staying in Ireland will make you a target of both sides. One of them will eventually find you, for your infamy is a prodigious motivator for them." Father Doran shuddered at the thought of succeeding in this quest. "We can find a role for you to add some goodness to this world. That's a penance better than any prayer can bring."

"Can I go to Australia? Is that possible?" Infused with this new hope, Theo straightened from a slouch. "I want to see my ma again."

"That may be possible. I will see what I can do."

Theo was grateful but still filled with guilt. They both left the confessional and embraced. Theo followed Father Doran to the rectory and then to one of the guest rooms. The priest assured him that he would be safe there while arrangements were made to get him out of Ireland.

Theo remained hidden in the rectory, not venturing out, waiting to learn what his mission was to be. During these days alone, he reflected on the past ten years.

Theo began to feel that Father Doran's penance was not enough for him. He needed to do his own penance. He decided that he would not run from the Brotherhood. He would meet with them face to face, to tell them he was leaving. He was no coward. He did not, of course, disclose this plan to Father Doran, who would never approve of it, who would tell him what he already knew: It was a suicidal plan.

Theo left the rectory after Father Doran began his day. He knew the priest would say early-morning mass, then make rounds at the hospital, then visit parishioners who were unable to leave their cottages, and then head off to teach classes all day. This schedule gave Theo hours to lay the groundwork for his plan.

He first headed off to the Avoca mines. He wore a hood and pulled it down to cover much of his face. His bushy beard took care of the rest. He wanted to make sure none of the miners recognized him—which was unlikely after ten years, but it was still better to be cautious.

He waited near the mine entrance until a particular miner arrived and strolled toward him, unaware, a dusty dented lunch pail in his hand. "Cole," Theo said quietly as the miner walked by him.

After a moment—and after Theo pulled his hood back somewhat—Cole seemed to recognize him. The miner's eyes grew large, his eyebrows arched high, and he gasped before replying: "The O'Neil?"

"Aye, 'tis me."

"The Brotherhood has everyone out looking for you"—Cole's head scanned left and right with fear—"and if they find you, I don't think they mean to buy you a Guinness."

"Aye, I am sure they mean me harm, but I am not afraid." He shrugged nonchalantly, already accepting his fate. "Nor do I regret my choice."

"What do you want from me? I don't want to get between you and the Brotherhood." Cole audibly gulped. "That's the least safe place in all of Ireland."

"Just give them a message for me. I want to meet in person. Have them arrange a place and time." He reached out and grabbed Cole's shirt, bringing him closer. "I will return here tomorrow to get their answer from you. But if they try to ambush me here, I will disappear." He released Cole's shirt, still staring at him, and pushed him toward the mine entrance. "Let them know I will meet anywhere, on their terms."

"Aye" was Cole's hushed reply as he hurried through the mine gates.

Theo returned to the rectory and continued his time in limbo. He spent the rest of the day reading, thinking, and exercising.

Father Doran returned later that day, carrying a small package. From a curtained window Theo watched him slowly walking up the sidewalk toward the rectory. The priest paused just before climbing the stairs. Theo could tell that there was something heavy on his shoulders. Maybe his secret group had refused Theo's request to go to Australia.

Father Doran went directly to Theo's room and knocked. Sitting on the bed, Theo braced himself for whatever news the priest was bringing. "Enter, Father."

Father Doran entered and sat next to Theo on the bed. "I have some news from Australia."

"Don't you mean *about* Australia?"

"No, son," the priest replied. He took Theo's hand in one of his and handed Theo a letter with the other. "It's news from Australia about your ma."

Theo took the letter, still confused, opened it, and began to read.

Dear Theo,

My name is Lily, and I am serving time with your ma at the penal colony in Australia. We have become close friends. I know I would not have survived here were it not for your ma's strength and kindness. I am writing this letter for her, as she is too weak to write it. She developed the consumption, and it has rapidly progressed. The authorities are allowing us to send you this for compassionate reasons, as they know she does not have much time left. By the time you read this letter, her suffering will be over, and she will return to our heavenly Father. She asked me to tell you that her love for you has never faltered. She also wanted to give you this medallion. She tells me it was your da's. She wore it around her neck and never took it off until now. She wanted me to tell you to follow its message and never waver from it. I don't know Gaelic, so I am not sure what it means. Knowing your ma, I am sure it is an important and meaningful message for you both.

Your ma is my dearest friend, and I don't know how I will make it through the next two years without her.

Sincerely, Lily

Theo folded the letter silently and placed it on the nightstand. Father Doran squeezed Theo's hand and waited for a reaction, but there was only silence. After a long pause, Father Doran said, "I think your ma knew that I could be trusted to find you, so she sent this to the school, addressed to me." He handed Theo the medallion. "She trusted me to make sure you got this. *'Bi daingean agus fas i dtreo an tsolais.'* It's a beautiful phrase. I am sure your da would be happy that you are trying to bend back to the light."

"Maybe," Theo replied. "But did I wait too long?" He placed the medallion over his head and slipped it under his shirt. Then he turned toward Father Doran. "There is nothing for me in Australia now. Can I change my plan? I want to go to America."

Father Doran nodded and left the room, feeling that Theo needed time alone to process this terrible news.

No watery tears spilled across Theo's cheeks, but inside tears of red fury filled his soul again. He contemplated how the Brotherhood had used his anger to control him for their own purposes. Now, as a grown man, he understood that they were just as evil as the English government.

Theo went to the mines the following day to meet Cole. He waited in the shadows, as before, until he saw the man approach. Cole handed him a slip of paper, then said, "They will meet you at that time and place. I did what you asked. Now I don't want to ever see you again." Cole turned his back and walked through the gate.

Theo stuffed the paper into his coat pocket, turned, and walked away, leaving the Avoca mines and their memories behind forever. When he returned to the rectory, he read what was written on the slip of paper. He was to meet the masked stranger in two days at a remote cottage outside of Wicklow. Theo knew of it, as it had served as a safe house for the Brotherhood members. He had heard it mentioned from time to time over the past few years. They were to meet at ten p.m., which meant the Brotherhood wanted to make sure there would be no witnesses.

Theo snuck out of the rectory after midnight. He needed the cover of darkness for the task at hand. He had some preparations to make at the cottage before the meeting. He had made a firm decision that if he were to die, it would not be in vain; he would take the masked stranger with him.

His first stop was the cave. Next he walked out to the abandoned cottage. He stayed a distance away to survey it before approaching. He wanted to be sure no one was present. Once assured it was quiet, he walked up to it. He laid the groundwork needed for the meeting and then returned to the rectory.

On the day of the scheduled meeting, Father Doran arrived with news. "Theo, arrangements have been made for you to be on a ship to America tomorrow." He then handed Theo an envelope.

Theo took the envelope, thinking that the timing could not have been better. If he survived tonight, he would be out of Ireland the following day. He opened the envelope to find a first-class ticket to America on the steamship *Star of the Sea* along with five hundred pounds.

Theo was stunned by the generosity of his sponsors. "Father, I cannot accept this money. It's too much." He tried to hand the money over to the priest. "I could never pay this back."

With on opened hand, Father Doran pushed the money back toward Theo. "It's not a gift. They expect you to work for it."

Theo's eyebrows raised. "What do they want me to do?"

Father Doran gestured for Theo to sit down. "The group I work for is very supportive of workers' rights both here and in America. They work with a fiery Irish-born labor organizer named Mary Harris Jones as well as union leaders to get workers out from under their greedy corporate overlords. They have used their influence and money to support strikes in America." He stood and paced around the room with his hands behind his back. "They feel that you can offer them something even more valuable. You can be their representative there to help organize labor unions."

"But I don't know anything about organizing unions. I wouldn't know where to start."

"Theo, I know that you have a unique set of skills. You are smart, resourceful, and attentive to what is important. We know that once you take on this task, you will not give up on it until victory. You are the best person for this job." He chuckled then. "And your reputation—let's say, your infamy—will put a little fear into those you come up against. I can assure you that the story of The O'Neil is already being talked about in America among the Irish immigrants."

Theo was shocked at this revelation. He had been happy that his new life might bring something positive as he left the darkness behind, but apparently his reputation would be following him. "I was hoping for a clean start in America, Father."

"It will be a clean start, but you know that rumors in Ireland travel faster than any ship or telegram. There's nothing any of us can do about that, so we might as well use it to our benefit."

Theo nodded silently.

"We will get you to the docks in Dublin tomorrow to board your ship to America." Father Doran stopped pacing in front of the window as if he could see the docks from there. "A union boss will be waiting for you at the docks in New York. He will have further instructions for you then. The group will make sure to place you somewhere needed."

"Thank you, Father." He bowed toward Father Doran, barely holding back tears. "I will do my best."

After Father Doran left the room, Theo lay on his bed and tried to imagine how his future would unfold. He slept for a while, knowing that the coming night would be a long one. He wondered if he would survive it to have a future at all.

Theo left the rectory around nine p.m. and walked out to the cottage for the meeting. He paused outside the low wall surrounding it, took a deep breath, and walked forward. He entered through a door that was barely hanging on by a single hinge.

"Well, if it isn't The O'Neil, come out of the shadows with the rats."

Theo just stared coldly. Standing next to the masked stranger was a red-haired mountain of a man, his face hidden by a bushy beard, holding a pistol that was pointed at him.

Theo didn't break his stare. He showed no fear because he felt none. "I am out. I am leaving the Brotherhood and Ireland."

The masked stranger laughed heartily. His thug remained stone-faced. "No one leaves the Brotherhood. Especially no one with the talents you possess." The thug cocked his pistol in anticipation of being able to silence this traitor once and for all. "You could ask Mickey what happens to people who betray the Brotherhood," the masked stranger continued. "Unfortunately, however, he seems to have disappeared."

Theo grinned, then said, "Well, if I am not leaving this cottage, then no one is."

This time the thug laughed at the ridiculousness of Theo's declaration while also looking forward to the chance to prove him wrong.

131

Theo made sure he was near the wire he had hidden in the cottage. A simple pull set his plan in motion. Everything happened in a flash. A loud explosion from behind the cottage caught the masked stranger and the thug off guard. They reflexively turned toward the sound. Theo darted forward toward his executioner, grabbed the gun with his left hand, and punched into the man's now-exposed neck. The thug released the gun and began to fall, making grunts that were more porcine than human.

The masked stranger reached into his waistband to retrieve his own pistol. In a continuous, fluid motion, Theo spun to his left and kicked the man's mid-section. The gun dropped to the floor as the masked stranger bent in half. Theo now had the thug's gun, which he brought down hard on the back of the man's head, laying him prostrate. Unlike his partner, this man did not grunt, as the crowning he'd received was kingly.

Theo dropped the gun to the floor, walked through the door, and retraced his path to the street. Before turning left onto the street, along the low rock wall, he located the second wire he had hidden, and he pulled it. As he passed along the tree line beside the street, a second explosion destroyed the cottage and everything in it. The blast blew leaves and debris all around him. He smiled, not because he had just killed his enemies, but because he had survived. His timing—along with the detonator wires he had prepared—had again been perfect.

By the next morning, word would already be spreading that The O'Neil might be the first person to get out of the Brotherhood alive and not in jail. The Irish grapevine would be buzzing for a while. But Father Doran surprised the returning Theo by greeting him at the door of the rectory. "Busy night, eh, Theo?" He suspected that Theo had executed some kind of plan, although not knowing the specifics as of yet.

"Aye, Father," he replied sheepishly.

The priest stepped aside and swept his left arm into the rectory in a welcoming move.

Theo nodded and walked inside.

Father Doran, ignoring what he assumed Theo had been doing, entered as well and closed the door. "I have you leaving for America tomorrow morning. You need to be at the dock by eight o'clock. The ship leaves at nine."

"That's good timing, Father." He couldn't help but smirk. "For tomorrow is a good time for me to leave Ireland."

Father Doran just said, "Yes, 'tis."

Theo slept surprisingly well, the moonlight creating shadows of his past life on the walls and in his dreams.

After leaving the early-morning carriage they had taken to Dublin, Theo walked silently with Father Doran toward the docks. Once there, the two embraced. Then Theo walked up the plank onto the Star of the Sea. As he reached the ship's rail, Theo turned, grabbed hold of his medallion, and nodded back to Father Doran.

The only thing Theo knew for sure at this point was that he was leaving the darkness behind him forever.

THE O'NEIL

A NOVEL

The Ship

Theo wended his way to his first-class stateroom, across the crowded deck, with the help of a porter. The porter opened the door to the room, and Theo stepped inside. The porter left with a coin snuggled in his fist as Theo closed the door behind him. He then surveyed the room he had been assigned: a rather comfortable-looking bed, a dresser, and a desk. On the wall was a small porthole that looked back toward Ireland. He felt a surge of guilt to have such amenities available to him.

On the bed was a note with a small candle lying on top of it. It was from Father Doran.

Theo,

The past darkness is forgiven. Now it is time to find the light.

Father Doran

He placed the note and candle aside, hoping he could forgive himself as easily as Father Doran had forgiven him. He lay down on the bed, lost in the thoughts of his past as it collided with his unknown future.

He was too restless to sleep, however, and he took it as a sign when the ship's horn blasted three times as it pulled away from the dock to give up his attempt at rest. He sat on the edge of the bed for a few minutes in silence. Then he walked down the hall and climbed the narrow stairs to the deck.

The railing around the deck was filled with passengers, most dressed in ill-fitting Irish country clothing. These were apparently Irish farmers and tenants leaving Ireland behind. How much sacrifice had been required of them to be able to even afford passage in steerage? Another pang of guilt.

Moving to a small gap on the port side, Theo nodded silently to his neighbors. He joined them in staring back at their old home country as it receded and shrank. No one said a word, but more than a few tears fell into Dublin Bay that day. They all stayed until the coast was nothing but a memory.

A seaman then came around to corral the steerage passengers back below. Steerage tickets allowed only limited time on deck, whereas first-class passengers had complete freedom to spend time on the deck, weather permitting. The typical first-class passenger didn't want to have the steerage souls interfering with his or her view. When the seaman approached Theo to ask to see his ticket, he felt a little relief. At least, he did not look like a first-class passenger.

As the steerage passengers filed by him on their way below, Theo watched, and that is when he saw her for the first time: A petite woman, with bright green eyes and flaming red hair blowing in the breeze. She walked right in front of him, but apparently, she was not as interested in him as he was in her. She didn't bat an eye, nor did her head even slightly deviate toward him. Then she was swallowed into the bowels of the ship.

Theo's guilt made even the comfortable bed in his stateroom feel hard. He spent as much time as he could on the deck. His first-class ticket allowed him this benefit, something he knew steerage passengers would have greatly appreciated.

One morning, around sunrise just a few days into the trip, he woke from another fitful sleep. He gave up trying to sleep more and went up to the deck. The rising sun blasted breathtaking colors across the sky in contrast to the cool solitude of the deck. As he stood gaping in awe at the sunrise, he felt a presence beside him. "'Tis beautiful," the red-haired woman with the green eyes said.

"Aye." Theo searched for more words to say.

The woman spoke again: "I have seen you up here before. It was the day we left."

A NOVEL

"It was indeed the day we left. I noticed you but didn't think you saw me in such a crowd."

"Let's just say that you are hard to miss." She gave him a mischievous grin, looking him directly in the eyes.

"My name is The O'Neil, but you can call me Theo." He bowed slightly and tipped the hat on his head that was not there.

"Well, Theo, it is certainly nice to make your acquaintance." She gazed at him with a warmth that Theo had not felt in a very long time. "The O'Neil is an interesting name. I'd like to hear the story behind it."

"I will be glad to tell you that story sometime, but right now I'd rather know your name."

"Laoise."[12]

It was the utterance of that simple word. At that very moment Theo fell in love. He knew Gaelic, so he knew that her name meant light. He knew this was either fate or the hand of God playing some role. He was speechless for a moment, just gazing into her bright green eyes. Once he got his breath back, he said, "That is the most beautiful name I have ever heard."

Her mischievous grin broadened into a bright smile. "Thank you. That is one of the nicest things anyone has said to me in a long time. So, tell me, Theo, why are you on this ship? Besides the obvious of going to America."

"Let's just say that I am running from the darkness."

She nodded her head slightly before saying, "That's interesting because I am running toward the light. I have been chased by the darkness for my entire life but was cunning enough to keep it just one pace behind me. I can show you how to do that if you'd like. It will take a fair amount of time, for with that comes my story as well. I very much want to tell you my story."

---

12 Pronounced "Lee-sha."

137

Theo drank in her every word, each one a note of the most beautiful music he could imagine. He delighted in learning this little bit about her history, and he was eager to learn so much more. Now he felt his knees buckle. Actually, only one knee, which bent down to the deck. He took one of Laoise's hands and looked up at her green eyes. "I know I just met you, but I can feel your light. A light that I sorely need." He cleared his throat. "Will you marry me?"

Laoise paused a few seconds, a pause that seemed like an eternity to Theo. Then: "The O'Neil, I would love to share my light with you! Yes!"

Theo stood, and they embraced and kissed for the first time. As they broke their embrace, they both started to laugh. Each was just as surprised as the other by their rash decision, yet they both knew it was destiny.

"You know," she said, catching her breath after their laughter subsided, "we are on a ship for the next month. I have not seen any churches nearby."

"Aye, but on a ship the captain is as good as having the pope with us."

Laoise laughed, and they embraced again. They couldn't keep their hands off each other.

Eventually, Laoise said, "I'd invite you back to my room, but it is filled with many spying eyes, some of those eyes attached to rats."

"I know you are traveling in steerage."

"Aye."

"Well, I have a solution to that, Laoise. Would you accompany me to my room? I don't have any roommates."

They walked arm in arm down the stairs to Theo's stateroom and remained there for the rest of the day and through the ensuing night.

The following day they reached out to the captain, who was thrilled to have the job of parish priest. The boatswain and the quartermaster served as witnesses. It was a simple but beautiful ceremony at sunset. When the couple kissed, cheers rained down from the rigging and across the deck.

A NOVEL

The couple spent most of the rest of the journey in Theo's stateroom. They reveled in each other's company. It was during these hours that they shared more of their past lives and their hopes for the future. As Laoise learned of the summary execution of Theo's father, she had an idea: "I assume your ma had the benefit of burial by her friend Lily and the respect of obsequies. Your da, however, was deprived of that right. The English took that away from him. We need to give him that."

Theo's forehead crinkled in confusion. "How could we do that for him?"

"We will give him a funeral on the deck and a burial at sea. Just the two of us."

Theo loved the idea, and his mind went into a swirl of more ideas to honor his father.

They waited for the perfect calm morning, so that the light would fill the day, chasing away the darkness and shadows of the past. They performed their ceremony at the stern of the ship, facing back toward Ireland. At this point, Laoise felt that she knew John O'Neil nearly as well as she knew Theo, from the stories he had told of his da.

They both stood at the rail, looking toward Ireland. A wind was blowing. It was not a wind felt by Laoise or by anyone else on Earth, for it was a wind from within Theo. On that wind were carried the words his da had composed after learning of the death of his own father from the famine. His da had never written the words down, but he later recited them to Theo in memory of him. To remember. To be passed down the generations of the O'Neil clan. The words floated in Theo's mind and memories. As real and permanent as any words ever written on paper. The words now came awake and spilled out:

Farewell.

The gods give light
From the sun.
Warm and quiet
It streams down.

The hazel and oak
Know to take it in,
For nature spoke
Somehow to them.

Our skin burns,
Resisting the light,
As our soul yearns
To end the night.

Here's to those
Who absorb the light
And to those who choose
To do what's right.

Farewell to you,
That soul so bright,
One of the few
Who could slay the night.

Laoise, stunned, stood silent, her vision blurred by the power of those words.

Theo then thought of something more to give his da. He turned to Laoise. "My da composed those words on hearing about the death of his father. He taught me that when I was a wee lad and said he wished he could play the fiddle, for he would have preferred to sing them as a song."

Laoise stepped closer to Theo and hugged him. Her tears fell onto his shoulder. His shirt drank them in like a remedy for his pain.

As they broke apart, Theo looked into her eyes and said, "Now an even better tribute. Those words in Gaelic:"

A NOVEL

> *Slán leat.*
>
> *Tugann na déithe solas*
> *Ón ngrian.*
> *Te agus ciúin*
> *Srutháin sé síos.*
>
> *An coll agus an darach*
> *Know a ghlacadh i,*
> *Do labhair nádúr*
> *Ar bhealach éigin dóibh.*
>
> *Dóitear ár gcraiceann,*
> *Resisting an solas,*
> *De réir mar a bhíonn ár n-anam ag iarraidh*
> *Chun deireadh a chur leis an oíche.*
>
> *Seo chugat siúd*
> *Go absorb an solas*
> *Agus iad siúd a roghnaigh*
> *Chun cad atá ceart a dhéanamh.*
>
> *Slán leat,*
> *An t-anam sin geal,*
> *Ceann de na cúpla*
> *D'fhéadfadh sé sin an oíche a mharú.*

When he finished, Theo lifted the medallion from around his neck.

Laoise looked at him with shock. She knew what the medallion meant to him. She put her hand on his forearm to stop him. "Theo, no."

Theo looked into her eyes and said with a sad sincerity, "My da was pure light, and I don't deserve this. You, Laoise, are my light now, and I don't need the medallion anymore." He lifted the medallion up to his eye level and watched it swing to and fro, like the pendulum of a clock. "This medallion represents my da, and since I never had the chance to bury his body in the Earth, I will inter the closest thing that I have to him. I will bury him at sea." With one hand holding the medallion, the other pressed against his chest, he continued: "From now on I need only to carry his memory. Until the day I die, he will live with me there."

Laoise let go of his arm and nodded. They each took one side of the leather thong and dropped it together into the sea. They stood silently, gazing out toward the sun rising over the horizon, beyond which was the Ireland they had left. They remained that way for several minutes, then turned and slowly walked back to their stateroom with arms wrapping each other.

They spent most of the rest of the journey together in the stateroom. They made a point, however, to enjoy the ocean views whenever the weather permitted. Theo felt a happiness that he'd thought he would never feel again. It was like the happiness of his childhood.

When they were just days from docking in New York, Laoise announced, "Theo, I want to tell you something. I might be with child."

"How can you know so early?"

"I just know. My period is late, and I have been sneaking up to the deck the past few mornings to vomit over the rail. So, I am fairly certain."

Theo yelped and grabbed his wife into a hug that lifted her off her feet. "I am so excited! I thought I had found as much happiness as was possible, but you just doubled it!"

Laoise smiled broadly as they held each other and just dissolved into one.

The Dock

As the ship neared New York Harbor, the excited passengers crowded up to the deck rail. The rules were relaxed to allow even the steerage passengers up on the deck with the first-class passengers. The anticipation in the air was palpable. They had survived their long journey.

Theo and Laoise had arrived at the rail early, baggage in hand, to make sure to get a prime position. As the shoreline grew, both were overcome with emotions. Laoise whispered to herself, "Pog mo thoin."

Theo could not help but laugh. He had heard Laoise utter this same phrase many times during the few weeks that he had known her. He figured out that this was her most-used expletive. The phrase reminded him so much of his mother each time she uttered it. In fact, it is the only one that he ever heard her say. "Yes, indeed!" he shouted as he turned toward his wife and wrapped his arms around her. "We've made it to America!"

Then they just silently stared at this strange new world, both wondering what the future might hold for them.

Once the ship docked and the gangway was locked into place, the passengers began to file out. The dock was crowded with people from all around the world, dressed in the clothes of their homelands and speaking a variety of languages. Theo and Laoise elbowed their way through the crowd. Even with their hands holding each other, it was difficult to stay together, due to the force of the humanity around them.

Theo suddenly felt a strong pull on his arm and quickly turned back in a panic. He calmed once he realized it was Laoise trying to get his attention. She had a smile on her face as she gazed upward, inviting his eyes to the same location. He edged toward her. "Are you all right?"

"I'm fine, but I just thought of a name for our baby." She pointed upward with her free hand. "If it is a girl, that is."

Theo followed her pointed hand toward the bow of the ship they had just disembarked from. On the side of the bow, painted in big white letters, was *The Star of the Sea*.

"Molly!" Theo shouted, using the Gaelic for the ship's name. "It's the perfect name!"

They both smiled and kissed briefly as the crowd bounced off them. They were corralled onto a barge by a New York City constable to be taken to Castle Garden, where immigrants would be processed and cleared to enter the United States. The remained on the barge for a long time while the *Star of the Sea* was inspected, rosters reviewed, and passengers counted. The anxiety of those passengers grew with every minute—both from the excitement of starting a new life as well as the dread of being rejected. Finally, the barge took them to the depot pier, where they disembarked. They were then ushered into the rotunda of Castle Garden, where they waited on wooden benches to be processed. They received a medical exam, which Laoise and Theo passed, along with most of the others. There were many services offered in Castle Garden, from transportation, letter writing with interpreters available in many different languages, and money exchange for American dollars.

Theo and Laoise needed only the money exchange, so they were among the first to leave the castle. Baggage in tow, they were confronted by another throng of people, some waiting and others moving toward their destination.

"Let's keep moving. The union boss is supposed to meet us here. They said he would find me, but we must get out of this crowd first."

They continued to push through toward the end of the dock as the crowd began to thin. It was then that Theo saw a short, broad man wearing a fancy suit with a bowler on his head. He was waving frantically. They headed toward him.

The man approached them with purpose. When he was adjacent, he reached out his hand toward Theo. "The name's Rafferty. You must be The O'Neil."

As Theo shook his hand, he replied, "Aye, I am The O'Neil, and this is my wife, Laoise."

Rafferty stammered a bit, then said, "A wife! I thought you were traveling alone. Well, no matter." He removed his bowler and gave an exaggerated bow toward Laoise. "Pleased to make your acquaintance, Laoise." He straightened and abruptly turned as he placed his bowler back on his bald pate, indicating that these brief pleasantries were over and it was time to get back to business. "Follow me. I have a carriage waiting for us."

The couple followed with their cases in hand to the waiting carriage. The horseman stowed their baggage as the trio entered the carriage and sat.

"I can't tell you how exciting it is to finally meet The O'Neil!" Rafferty exclaimed. "You already have quite the reputation here in America. The man who fought the English and escaped from the Brotherhood! Not many can say they accomplished that." He wiggled in his seat across from Theo and Laoise, as if planting himself deeper into the cushion. "Your name carries some weight around here, and that is just what we need to get the coal union going."

Father Doran had already prepared Theo for his reputation being so strong in America, but hearing the proof from Rafferty made him a bit forlorn. It was clear that his past had indeed followed him to America. He knew the Irish grapevine was world-famous, but he hadn't realized how fast and wide those vines grew. He hoped he could turn that into something positive.

Rafferty continued: "We have everything in place for you to start working as a coal miner. We planned on setting you up with housing, but I was informed that you preferred to start in company housing. Is that true?"

"Aye, I want to live like the other miners starting out. I feel it's important to fully understand their plight. Once we get settled, we may get our own place, but I will pay for it out of my wages and the generous gift I was given back in Ireland."

Rafferty nodded toward Laoise. "I understand your reasoning, but those quarters are not the most comfortable or private."

"We'll manage," replied Laoise, realizing that comment had been directed toward her.

Then Theo spoke: "You haven't yet told us *where* we are going."

Laoise gulped. Once the answer was given, their situation would be real; it would no longer be merely a plan or an idea.

Rafferty said, "Scranton!"

Laoise said, "Pog mo thoin!"

Theo asked, "Scranton, where the feck is that?"

A NOVEL